STUDIES IN THE SERMON ON THE MOUNT

STUDIES IN THE SERMON ON THE MOUNT

By

OSWALD CHAMBERS

Author of "Bible Psychology" "The Cure oft Souls/' etc. Principal of London Bible Training College.

"We may all be disciples; why should we not be scholars of the one Teacher? Come, let Him lure thee—give up all other teachers and hear this Teacher sent from God."

J. PARKER

KALPAZ

ISBN: 978-93-5128-420-8(PB)

First Published in 1915
Indian Reprint in 2017

Published by

Kalpaz Publications
C-30, Satyawati Nagar,
Delhi – 110052
E-mail: kalpaz@hotmail.com
Website: kalpazpublications.com
Ph.: +91-9212142040

FOREWORD

In his Sixth Study our author says, "Jesus warns His disciples to test preachers and teachers by their fruit. There are two ways of testing by fruit—one by the fruit in the life of the preacher, and the other is by the fruit in the life of the doctrine." It is a genuine joy to be able to apply these touchstones of character and teaching to the life and words of Oswald Chambers.

It was the writer's rare privilege to be in the same home with him and to sit under his ministry for a number of months; to see him daily and to find in him a patient counselor, an exemplary as well as trustworthy teacher, and a Christlike friend. The following words are none too vividly descriptive of this modern prophet teacher:

> "Who never sold the truth to serve the hour,
> Nor paltered with eternal God for power,
> Who let the turbid stream of rumor flow
> Thro' either babbling world high or low;
> Whose life is work, whose language rife
> With rugged maxims hewn from life,
> Who never spoke against a foe"

And as to the second test proposed, "the fruit... of the doctrine"—will there be found in all the Church of Christ of today one whose words are more weighty with spiritual values? "But," says some simple soul, "I don't understand him." The more is the pity. Leave then the evening newspaper, the book of religious wonder-tales, the high-flown writings "watered" with adjectives. but empty of thought or power, and read these pages again and again until the truth "soaks" through to your innermost consciousness. There is about us a flood of profession, but a failure in possession; a torrent of criticism for those who "follow not us," but a trickling rivulet of sound advice to ourselves. To heed the words of our Lord's Sermon on the Mount as interpreted by Oswald Chambers will transform holiness people into holy people, and faithless verbosity into Christian humility. Unto which glorious result, God speed the day!

—J. F. K.

CONTENTS.

Study Number One

N. B. (1) Introductory note on the Gospel according to St. Matthew and St. Luke respectively.

(2) The student is advised to get a copy of Dr. Gore's "The Sermon on the Mount."

ST. MATTHEW: COLLECTION OF DISCOURSES.

1. Address to the Twelve.
   Matthew 5: 1-16, 39-42, 44-48; 7: 1-6; 12: 15-17.
2. Address on Prayer.
   Matthew 6: 9-15; 7: 7-11.
3. Answer to a Theological Question.
   Matthew 7: 13, 14; 8: 11, 12.
4. Address on Worldly-mindedness.
   Matthew 6: 19-34.
5. Address in the Synagogue of Capernaum.
   Matthew 5: 17-39, 43; 6: 1-8, 16-18.

ST. LUKE: CHRONOLOGICAL DIVISIONS.

1. Address to the Twelve.
   Luke 6: 20: 20-28, 41-49; 11: 32.
2. Address on Prayer.
   Luke 11: 1-13.
3. Answer to a Theological Question.
   Luke 13: 23-30.
4. Address on Worldly-mindedness.
   Luke 12: 13-34.
5. Address in the Synagogue of Capernaum.
   Luke 4: 31-37; (Mark 1: 21-28).

STUDY NUMBER ONE.

In order to understand the Sermon on the Mount, it is necessary to know the mind of the Preacher, and this knowledge can be gained by anyone who will receive the Holy Spirit. (Luke 11:13; John 20:22; Acts 19:2.)

Beware of placing our Lord Jesus as a teacher first instead of a Savior. We must first know Him as a Savior before His teachings have any meaning for us, or before they have any other meaning than that of an ideal which leads to despair. There are some people who take up this attitude: "I do not believe there is any necessity to preach an atonement through Jesus Christ, I do not believe it is necessary to say He died for our sins, I believe that Jesus is a teacher only." That attitude is very prevalent to-day, but it is a very absurd as well as dangerous one, for if He was only a teacher, His teaching would produce despair. Fancy coming to men and women with defective lives and defiled hearts and wrong mainsprings and telling them to be pure in heart! What would be the good of His giving us an ideal that we could not possibly come near? we are happier without knowing it. If Jesus is only a teacher, then all He can do is to tantalise us, to erect a standard we cannot attain to; but if we know Him first as Savior, if we are born again of the Spirit of God, we know that He did not come to teach us only, but that He came to make us what He teaches we should be.

The Gospel according to St. Matthew, in its original state in the early Church, was in two sections. One section was composed of five great discourses of our Lord's with no historical narrative at all. This was transcribed by Matthew himself. The second section has the five discourses fitted into the historical narratives of our Lord's life. The latter was compiled by a student-evangelist of Matthew's, and it is this latter Gospel that we know.

Matthew wrote his Gospel according to topics; Luke, a cultured physician, an evangelist and disciple of Paul's, wrote his Gospel in the perfect manner of the Greek historians, so that the student who wants to know where the various teachings of Jesus are to be placed in our Lord's life must turn to Luke's Gospel.

"The Sermon on the Mount" is the title given by Matthew to a collection of discourses by our Lord, only one of which was literally preached on the mountain, the others were preached in the mountainous district. The evangelists Matthew, Peter, Paul and John took incidents out of the life of our Lord on which they based their doctrines, and the four Gospels are simply the records of their preaching under the guidance of the Holy Spirit. It sounds very precarious to us to say that it was all trusted to memory and oral transmission, but when we remember there was a kind of curse given by the rabbis to anyone who put anything in writing, and if a student in a rabbinical school made a slip in memory he was supposed to be worthy of death, it alters our too hasty first conclusions about the matter. These early disciples were brought up in that school, and when Paul talks about the "deposit" that Timothy had, this is what he is alluding to. They were all trained to retain accurate details and descriptions of our Lord's life; and in the year 62 or 65 Matthew wrote his Gospel.

The four Gospels are four contrasted views of our Lord's life, not contradictory views. The astute mind behind the Gospels is not a human mind at all, but the Holy Ghost. "Holy men wrote as they were moved by the Spirit of God." A "harmony of the Gospels" is a rather mistaken idea; harmony must imply discord as well as accord. The very same principle holds in understanding the unity of the Gospels as in understanding our Lord's teachings, viz., a personal knowledge of the mind of the Lord, which can be obtained by receiving the Holy Spirit. Peter says that holy men wrote as they were moved, he did not say holy machines. You will find that God the Holy Ghost instead of effacing the individuality of these men did exactly the opposite, He lifted their personality to a point of "white heat," so to speak, and used it as the means of presenting the Gospel of God. The more you brood over that line of things the more you will be able to discard the *cheap and hasty* criticism which is honeycombing so much of the teaching nowadays. You will find as many points in the Gospel that won't fit into another as you find points that will. The word we need is not harmony in the Gospels, but *unity,* and the unity is by the Holy Ghost.

(1) ADDRESS TO THE TWELVE.

When our Lord ordained twelve men out of the multitude that followed Him He preached to them what we have in Matthew 5 and 7, and He began by saying, "Blessed are," and then He must have staggered them by what followed. They were to be blessed in every particular which they had been taught from their earliest childhood was a curse. The statements of Jesus seem so wonderfully simple, but in reality they are like spiritual torpedoes, they explode and burst in the unconscious mind, and they come up to our conscious mind and we say, "What a startling statement that is!" Our Lord was talking to Jews, and the Jews believed, down to their joints and marrow, that the sign of the blessing of God was material prosperity in every shape and form, and Jesus says, "Blessed are ye" for exactly the opposite.

We must remember that Jesus wrote nothing, He spoke everything, and to look upon His teachings as a written act of Parliament is absurd, and to look upon His statements as isolated texts to be mechanically followed is equally misleading. Our Lord expects that these statements of His will be carried out in the lives of these men in the power of the Spirit He is to give them. There are two ways of looking at the Sermon on the Mount: a number of teachers to-day say that it was a forecast of what is going to be during the Millennium and it has no application whatever to us now. There are others who say that it has only an application to us now and has no reference to any other time. Now both those views are right, but either alone is wrong. In this present dispensation, Jesus says the kingdom of God is inside men, and men are called upon to live out His Spirit and His teaching in an age that will not recognize Him. That spells limitation and very often disaster. In the next dispensation the kingdom of God will be established outside as well as inside men. These two points of view are always put together in the New Testament.

(2) ADDRESS ON PRAYER.

Our Lord begins His teaching about prayer with a little playful irony in which He tells them to watch their motives (Matt. 6:5), "Why do you want to pray? Do you want to be known as a praying man? Well, verily that is your reward, you will be known as a praying man, but there is no more to it, there is no answer to your prayer." The next thing He told them was to keep a secret relationship between themselves and God (Matt. 6:6), and in verse 7 He told them not to rely on their own earnestness when praying. These three statements of Jesus, which are so familiar to us, are revolutionary. Call a halt one moment and ask yourself, "Why do I want to pray, what is my motive? Have I a personal, secret relationship to God that nobody knows but myself? And what is my method when I pray, am I really relying on God or on my own earnestness?" These sayings of Jesus go to the very root of all praying. The majority of us make the blunder of depending on our own earnestness and not on God at all. It is confidence in Him. (1 John 5: 14, 15.) All our fuss, all our earnestness, all our "gifts of prayer" are not the slightest atom of use to Jesus Christ, He pays no attention to them. Our Lord gave His disciples the pattern prayer and supplied in that prayer their want of ideas and words and faith. Then He taught them the prayer of patience. Our Lord's instruction about patience in prayer conveys this lesson: "If you are right with God, and God delays the manifested answer to your prayer, don't misjudge Him, don't think of Him as an unkind friend, or an unnatural father, or an unjust judge, but keep at it. Your prayer will certainly be answered," says Jesus, "for everyone that asks receives," and "men ought always to pray and not faint." Your Heavenly Father will explain it all one day, He cannot just now because He is developing your character.

(3) ANSWER TO A THEOLOGICAL QUESTION.

Our Lord in His answers very rarely, if ever, appears to deal with the questions asked. In Luke 13 a very devout, pious individual asks Him if there be many saved or few, and Jesus gave him a reply in an Oriental proverb, the effect of which is, "See that your own feet are on the right path." At another time the disciples said, in a really earnest mood, "Lord, increase our faith," and Jesus quoted them an Oriental proverb about a grain of mustard seed and a mountain, which if you watch the setting, undoubtedly conveys this: "Get personally related to me, and lack of faith will never bother you." Whenever we lack faith, it is simply that we do not trust Him; faith must be the result of a personal understanding. Our Lord's answers seem at first to evade the point, but instead of evading it, He goes underneath the questions and puts something in that will solve every question. He never answers our shallow questions, but He deals with the great, unconscious need that made them arise. One class of questions our Lord never answered, those that come from the head, the reason being that no question from the head is ever original.

(4) ADDRESS ON WORLDLY-MINDEDNESS.

Our Lord in this discourse and in many others,

was strong on the necessity of a line of demarcation between worldly-mindedness and spirit-mindedness while we are in the world. We are most of us certain that we can serve two masters with a little skill and tact, but we sooner or later come to the conclusion that Jesus knows best. (There is all the difference between Heaven and Hell in that simple phrase, "Jesus knows best." Think what it means in your personal life, in your business life. Some of us are uncommonly like the disciples when Jesus was with them in the fishing boat, they thought in effect, "He is a carpenter, and doesn't know anything about fishing; He can go to sleep, He does not know anything about managing boats;" but when the storm comes on, Jesus is the only one who can manage the boat, the fishermen are terrified out of their wits. It is a great moment in a man's life when he realizes that Jesus knows more about his business than he does himself.)

Take our attitude to our Lord's statement that everyone that asks receives, the majority of us think we believe it, but our attitude really is, "I'll ask, but it may not be His will to answer," meaning that I have no confidence in Jesus further than my common sense allows me to go. We call ourselves Christians, but where do we place Jesus? We limit Him on the right hand and on the left, by trusting to ourselves. The man or woman who trusts Jesus in a definite, practical way ought to be freer than anyone else to do his or her business; free from fret and worry, they can go with absolute certainty into the daily life.

Jesus also taught that if men were to be spiritual, they must sacrifice the natural, that the only ground of the spiritual is on the basis of the sacrifice of the natural. One of the greatest principles—which we do not seem to grasp, but which was very evident in our Lord's life—is that the natural life is neither moral nor immoral. I make it moral or immoral. Jesus says the natural life is meant for sacrifice, we can give it as a gift to God, that is the way to become spiritual. Jesus says if we do not do that, we must barter the spiritual. That is where Adam failed, he refused to sacrifice the natural life and make it spiritual by obeying God's voice in it, consequently he sinned, the sin of his right to himself. If we say, "I like this natural life, I do not want to be a saint, I do not want to sacrifice the natural life for the spiritual," then Jesus says you must barter the spiritual. It is not a punishment, it is an eternal principle. If you are going to be spiritual, you must barter the natural, sacrifice it. Spirituality is not a sweet tendency towards piety in people who have not enough life in them to be bad; spirituality is the possession of the Holy Spirit of God which is, as it were, masculine in its strength, and that will make the most corrupt twisted, sin-stained life spiritual if He be obeyed.

(5) ADDRESS IN THE SYNAGOGUE.

Jesus distinctly says here that He is the meaning and the fulfillment of all the old commandments, and if any man says it does not matter whether you heed those commandments or not Jesus says that He condemns him. If the old commandments were difficult, our Lord's principles are fathoms deeper and more difficult. He actually says that unless the men who were His disciples exceeded all the good doings of the good people who are not His disciples, they will in no case enter the kingdom of Heaven. Think of the best men and women you know who have never received the Spirit of God and who make no profession—they are upright, sterling, noble and Jesus says in effect, "If you have received my Spirit and are my disciples, you have to exceed everything they do and are, or you will never see the kingdom of Heaven." Instead of the criticism of Christians being wrong, it is absolutely right; we have to *produce our goods up to* and have the life in us that Jesus said we would *sample*. If we are born again of the Holy Ghost, have by means of His cross, we have to show it by the way we talk, the way we act and transact our business.

The teaching in the Sermon on the Mount produces despair in the natural man, the one thing Jesus wants it to do, because immediately we get to despair we come to Jesus Christ like paupers, and are willing to receive from Him. "Blessed are the paupers in spirit"—that is the very first principle of the kingdom. As long as we have some conceited, self-righteous notion of our own—"Oh, yes, I can do this"—God has to allow us to go on until we break our ignorance over some obstacle, then we realize that, after all, Jesus knew best—"Blessed are the poor in spirit." It is receiving all the way along.

Jesus spoke these things openly to all men, not to a special clique, and if they are binding on any man they are binding on all equally.

This is a brief introduction to our more detailed study of the Sermon on the Mount. Pray that God's Spirit will illuminate these studies to you.

Study Number Two

MATTHEW FIVE.

A. DIVINE DISPROPORTION.

1. The "Mines" of God.
   Luke 6:20-26.

2. The Motive of Godliness.
   Matthew 5:11, 12.

B. DIVINE DISADVANTAGE.

1. Concentrated Service.
   Matthew 5:13.

2. Conspicuous Setting.
   Matthew 5:14-16.

C. DIVINE DECLARATION.

1. His Mission.
   Matthew 5:20.

2. His Message.
   Matthew 5:20.

N. B. A working exposition of the subconscious mind will be given in this lecture.

STUDY NUMBER TWO

MATTHEW 5.

We will take the note at the foot of the outline first. N. B. Every mind has two compartments: a conscious and an unconscious compartment. Subconscious simply means under consciousness. The things we hear and read slip away from our memory; we say, they do not really, they go into the unconscious mind. The work of the Spirit of God in a Christian is to bring back into our conscious mind the things that are stored in the subconscious. So in studying the Bible never go on the line that because you do not understand what you are reading just now it will be of no use; you find the habit of Bible study is to store the mind with Bible knowledge, and then perhaps after years when you come across something in your circumstances, the Spirit of God will bring back to your conscious mind something you never remembered you had, and you say, "I wonder wherever that came from!"

Always bear in mind this twofold aspect of the mind. There is nothing supernatural or marvellous in it in the sense of being uncanny, it is simply a knowledge of how God has made us. So it is foolish to estimate only by what we consciously understand at the time; we may not see any meaning in it for our lives, but if we store it away the Spirit of God will bring it back to our remembrance.

The Sermon on the Mount lays down the principles at the basis of our Lord's kingdom, and it is by these principles, which are purposely veiled as laws and conduct, that we understand the nature of the Kingdom. A principle is something that explains, and the principles of the Sermon on the Mount explain the character of our Lord's kingdom. It is by these principles alone that we understand His kingdom, but when it comes to personal conduct we find instantly God veils them.

The two methods of applying these principles to the conduct of individual Christians to-day—both of which are wrong—are first, the lax method, which makes out that these principles are mere poetry and nothing more. The other method is the literal one whereby the statements are applied literally. The first method makes out that society, as it is, is all right; the latter method makes out that it is all rotten. The one abiding method of interpretation is the Spirit of Jesus Christ in the heart of a believer bringing His principles to apply in the particular circumstances in which he is placed. (See Rom. 12:2.) The methods we have mentioned are dodges to get away from the sternness of Jesus Christ's requirements. If the Sermon on the Mount is to be applied literally, then any fool can do that, we do not need to be born again to do that. But Jesus Christ insists that if any man is going to partake of the character of His kingdom, he must have His nature, all we understand by being born again and sanctified. Then we have the responsibility, God does not take it, we have the responsibility of walking in the light and applying His principles to our circumstances. The whole thing is put in a nutshell by the apostle Paul: "Be renewed in the spirit of your mind, that you may prove what the will of God is, the thing that is acceptable and right and perfect."

A. Divine Disproportion. (Matt. 5: 1-12.)

(1) The "Mines" of God. (Luke 6:20-26.)

(2) The Motive of Godliness. (Matt. 5:11, 12.)

The Sermon on the Mount is quite unlike the

Ten Commandments, in the sense of its principles being absolutely unworkable unless Jesus Christ can remake us.

(1) The "Mines of God." (Luke 6:20-26.) I mean by "mines" an under-working charged with explosives. The first time you read the Beatitudes they appear beautiful and simple and unstartling, and they go unobserved into your subconsciousness. Then you come across something in your practical life whereby the Holy Ghost brings back one of these Beatitudes, and you find, to your astonishment, that it is like a spiritual torpedo, it "rips" and "tears" and revolutionizes everything you ever knew. The Beatitudes spring from the life blood of Jesus Christ, that is they contain all His meaning, and when we read them first they seem merely mild and beautiful precepts for all unworldly, useless people, and of very little practical use in the stern, workaday world in which we live. However, we soon find that these Beatitudes contain the dynamite of the Holy Ghost. In Luke's account (Luke 6: 20:-26) the Beatitudes are paralleled by the "Woes," which is an indication of how these principles of Jesus work. They explode, as it were, when the circumstances of life require them to do so. For instance, when you

find yourself suddenly faced by circumstances that praise you for your spiritual possessions, Beatitude 3 emerges into the conscious life like a veritable spiritual torpedo; or again, when your circumstances are finding you full of ecstacy and delight over spiritual service, Beatitude 4 comes into the life with staggering amazement. You cannot apply them literally. You allow the life of God, first of all, to invade you by regeneration and sanctification, and then as you have been soaking your mind in the teaching of Jesus, and it has been slipping down into the unconscious mind, then a set of circumstances arises where suddenly one of them emerges, and instantly you have to ask yourself, "Will I walk in the light of it? Will I accept the tremendous spiritual tornado which will be produced in my circumstances if I follow this teaching of Jesus? I have the power to follow it if I will!" That is the way the Spirit of God works. It always comes with astonishing discomfort to begin with, it is all out of proportion to our ways of looking at things, and we have slowly to form our walk and conversation in the line of His precepts.

(2) The Motive of Godliness. (Matt. 5: 11, 12.) The motive at the back of the precepts of the Sermon on the Mount is, first and foremost,

love for God. Not that the Beatitudes have no meaning in our relationship to men, that relationship is so obvious it scarcely needs noting, but the Godward aspect is not so obvious. Read the Beatitudes with your mind fixed on God. Put His name after every one of them, and you will realize the neglected side of the Beatitudes. "Blessed are the poor in spirit," towards God. "Blessed are the meek," towards God's dispensations. "Blessed are the merciful," to God's reputation. "Blessed are the pure in heart," that is obviously Godward. "Blessed are the peacemakers" (exactly the note that was struck at the birth of Jesus, a peace-making relationship between God and man). Is it possible to carry out the Beatitudes? Never! unless God can do what Jesus Christ says He can, give us the Holy Spirit, who will remake us and put us in a new realm. The Sermon on the Mount is a statement of the life we will live when the Holy Ghost is getting His way with us.

Our Lord says that His disciples are to rejoice on one condition, when they are reviled and persecuted and slandered for His sake. That is left out in modern Christian teaching, we are told that if we suffer for "conviction's sake," for "conscience's sake," it is all that is necessary. Peter says you do not do any more than other people if you only suffer that way. We have to suffer for "Jesus' sake:" that is, the whole motive underneath is to be well pleasing to God. The true blessedness of the saint is in determinedly making and keeping God *first*. Herein is the disproportion of Jesus Christ's principles and moral teaching, the reason being that Christ bases everything on God-realization, while other teachers base their teaching on self-realization. Whenever the Holy Ghost sees a chance of glorifying Jesus, He will take your heart, your nerves, your whole personality, and simply make them blaze and glow with a personal, passionate devotion and love to the Lord Jesus Christ; not devotion to a cause, not a devotee to a principle, but a devoted love-slave of the Lord Jesus Christ. No man on earth has that love unless the Holy Ghost has imparted it. (Rom. 5:5.) We may admire Him and respect Him and reverence Him, but we *cannot* love Him; the only lover of the Lord Jesus Christ is the Holy Ghost.

B. Divine Disadvantage. (Matt. 5:13-16.)

(1) Concentrated Service. (5:13.)

(2) Conspicuous Setting. (5:14-16.)

The disadvantage of a saint in the present condition of things is that he has to make the centre of his life, confession of Jesus, not in secret, but glaringly public. The tendency to be holy and say nothing about it is right from every standpoint but from the standpoint of the Holy Spirit. It is doubtless much to the advantage of Christian men and women in this age to keep quiet (that is, advantage from the self-realization standpoint), and the tendency is growing stronger, "Don't say anything about it; be a Christian, live a holy life, but do keep quiet."

(1) Concentrated Service. (5:13.) "Ye are the salt of the earth." Our Lord's picture of salt is terse and concise, for the most concentrated thing known to human beings is salt, it tastes like nothing else but salt every time and all the time. That is our Lord's illustration of a disciple. Salt preserves wholesomeness and prevents decay. The disciples of Jesus in the present dispensation preserve society from corruption. Some modern Christian teachers would like us to believe that Jesus said, "Ye are the sugar of the earth," meaning that gentleness and winsomeness without curativeness is the idea of a Christian. How are we to maintain the healthy, salty tang of saintliness? By remaining rightly related to God through Jesus Christ.

(2) Conspicuous Setting. (5:14-16.) The

things our Lord uses as illustrations, viz., light and a city set on a hill, are the most conspicuous things known to us, there is no possibility of mistaking them. Jesus says, "Be like that, in your home, in your business, in your church, conspicuously a Christian for ridicule or for respect according to the moods of the people you are with." Our Lord taught His disciples, in Matthew 10:16-28, the need to be conspicuous proclaimers of the truth, and not to cover it up for fear of wolfish men. Our Lord will have nothing of the nature of a covert disciple. These three things, salt, light and a city set on a hill, are things among men that cause the most annoyance as well as those that attract the vilest things. Salt, to preserve from corrupion, has very often to be placed in the midst of it and before it can do its work it causes excessive irritation, which spells persecution. Light attracts bats and hideous night-moths and points out the way for burglars as well as other people. Jesus would have us remember that men will certainly defraud us. A city is the gathering place for all the human driftwood that will not work for its own living, so the Christian will have any number of parasites and ungrateful "hangers-on." All these considerations form a powerful temptation to pretend we are not salt, to put our light under a bushel, and cover our city with a fog. You cannot soil light; you may attempt to grasp a beam of light with the sootiest hand, but you leave no mark on the light. You can soil a moral man or an innocent man, but you cannot soil a man or woman who is made pure by the Holy Ghost and who remains there; they are light. A sunbeam may shine into the filthiest hovel in the slums of a city, but it cannot be soiled. Thank God for the men and women who are spending their lives in the slums of the earth, not as moral characters to lift their brother men to cleaner styles, but as the light of God, pure and unspotted from the world, shining a way for the men to get back to God!

If we have been covering our light, uncover it! The light always reveals and guides and blazes, and men dislike it when their deeds are evil and prefer darkness.

C. Divine Declaration. (Matt. 5:17-20.)

(1) His Mission. (5:17-19.)

(2) His Message. (5:20.)

Here our Lord places Himself as the exact meaning and fulfillment of all the Old Testament commandments and prophecies. He says that His mission is to fulfill the law and the prophets, and further that any teacher in this present era that breaks the former laws and teaches men to do so because they belong to a former dispensation shall suffer severe impoverishment. All not ignored. There are teachers who say that former Old Testament laws are fulfilled in Christ, the Sermon on the Mount supersedes the Ten Commandments, and that because we are not under "law but under grace," it does not matter whether we honor our father and mother, whether we covet our neighbor's possessions, etc. Beware of statements like this: "There is no need now-a-days to observe giving the 'tenth,' either of money or of time, we are under a new dispensation and it all belongs to God." That, in practical application, means sentimental "dust-throwing." The giving of the tenth is not a sign that it all belongs to God, but a sign that the "tenth" belongs to God and the rest is ours, and we are held responsible for what we do with it. It is surprising how easily we can juggle ourselves out of Jesus Christ's principles by one or two pious principles repeated often enough. The only safeguard is to keep personally related to Him. 1 John 1:7 is the great safeguard for all spiritual understanding. "Walk in the light"—not the light of my convictions or theories, but the light God is in. Literal interpretation of the Sermon on the Mount is child's play; the interpretation by the Spirit of Christ is the stern work of a saint, and it requires all that the Lord kept teaching His disciples—Spiritual Concentration.

(2) His Message. (5:20.)

Our Lord's message here is that the righteousness of the scribes and Pharisees was right, not wrong, and that His disciples were to exceed that righteousness. That the Pharisees did much more and other than righteousness is obviously clear, but our Lord is here talking of their righteousness. What is it that exceeds right doing if it be not right being? Right being, without doing anything, is possible, but it cannot exceed the righteousness of the scribes and Pharisees. The way I can stop right doing is by refusing to enter into relationship with God, both by His words and providences. This is an aspect of things continually overlooked in Christian morality. The statement we so often hear, "If I were in your circumstances, I could be as good as you are," is perfectly true, but in your own circumstances you can do much better if the Spirit of God dwells in you. We are apt to think the charge is not true that, if they were in the circumstances we are in, they would be as good as we are. Of course they would, in all probability much better, but let us get hold of the secret that the harder the circumstances God's providence has brought around you, the brighter and grander does your light shine; the more difficult and perplexing the surroundings, the more difficult the people you have to deal with, the more God-glorifying is the exhibition of Christ's life in you. The monks in the Middle Ages refused to take the responsibilities of life; all they wanted was to be and not to do. They could not exceed the righteousness of the scribes and Pharisees; they shut themselves away from the world, and people to-day want to cut themselves off from this and that relationship. But Jesus Christ's message is that unless we exceed in *doing* (the Pharisees were nothing in *being*), we shall never enter the kingdom of God.

Verse 16 brings out the same meaning, "When men see your good works, they will glorify your Father in Heaven." If our Lord had meant in being only, He would not have used the word exceed, He would have said, "Except your righteousness be otherwise than."

Study Number Three

MATTHEW FIVE.

A. THE ACCOUNT WITH PURITY.

1. Disposition and Deeds.
   Matthew 5: 21, 22.

2. Temper of Mind and Truth of Manner.
   Matthew 5:23, 26.

3. Lust and License.
   Matthew 5: 27, 28.

4. Direction of Discipline.
   Matthew 5:29, 30.

B. THE ACCOUNT WITH PRACTICE.

1. Scandal.
   Matthew 5:31, 32.

2. Irreverent Reverence.
   Matthew 5:33-36.

3. Integrity.
   Matthew 5:37.

C. THE ACCOUNT WITH PERSECUTION.

1. Toward Insult.
   Matthew 5:38, 39.

2. Towards.Extortion.
   Matthew 5:40.

3. Towards Tyranny.
   Matthew 5:41, 42.

STUDY NUMBER THREE.

MATTHEW 5.

Our Lord here is laying down this principle that, if these disciples are going to follow Him and obey His Spirit, they have to lay their account with purity, with practice, and with persecution. Now purity is an intensely difficult thing to define. Purity is a state of heart on the inside which we can best define as being just like Jesus Christ's heart. You cannot make yourself pure by obeying laws. Our Lord shows how this heart purity works out. He takes, first of all, a parallel picture from the old law, and then shows how He interprets it from the pure-heart standard. It is not only a question of doing the things rightly, but of the doer on the inside being right.

(1) Disposition and Deeds. (5:21, 22.) Our Lord here is alluding to something that was quite familiar to the disciples. It was customary

for some people to totally disregard what was known as the common judgment, what we would call the ordinary law courts, and if they went too far they got into danger of an inner court (we have nothing quite like it in our law), and if they insisted on being contemptuous with that one, they were in danger of the final judgment, which meant they were flung out as wastrels and anarchists. Jesus uses that as a spiritual illustration, He puts it this way, that our disposition has to be like His, that our motive, *i. e.*, the place we cannot get at ourselves, must be right. Read Psalm 139 with this idea in mind. The Psalmist is realizing he is much too big for himself, that there are things he cannot get at, but that, just as God can understand the big world outside, He can understand the bigger world inside him. To the Psalmist the world is bigger on the inside than on the outside, and he says, "Now, Lord, search me out and see if there be any way of grief in me," and the Hebrew words mean, "Trace me out; the dreams of my dreams, the motives of my motives, make those right." That is what Jesus is alluding to here, the motives of my motives and the springs of my dreams must be so right that right deeds will naturally follow. Other teachers tell of certain things to suppress, certain rules and regulations to obey; Jesus Christ never gives us rules and regulations. Try, for instance, to use the Sermon on the Mount as a series of rules and regulations and you find you cannot do it. They are truths that can only be interpreted by a new spirit which Jesus Christ puts in. Jesus teaches that He can alter our mainspring of action. He does not teach us to curb or suppress the wrong disposition, He does not even give us something to counteract it, He gives us a totally new disposition. Every now and again that aspect of Jesus Christ's teaching which is so radical is being refined away by Christian teachers, they tell us that Jesus Christ cannot do what He says He can. They say, "Of course what the Lord meant was not what He said, but what I tell you," that He does not alter our disposition, but He puts something in us that counteracts the old disposition. That is a compromise with something Jesus never compromised with. The only way in which a Christian knows that Jesus has given him a pure heart is by *trying* circumstances. This is the way it works; you are brought under trying circumstances, people imply wrong motives to you, and if the Lord has made your heart pure, you are the most astonished person in the world, because, instead of feeling resentment, you feel exactly the opposite, you feel a most amazing difference inside. That is the only proof we have according to the Sermon on the Mount that God has altered the heart, not that we persuade ourselves He has done it, but that we prove it. When circumstances put us to the test, we say, "Why, bless God! this is a marvelous alteration, I know now He has altered me because before I would have got sour and irritable and sarcastic and spiteful." Our Lord goes behind the old law to the disposition.

(2) Temper of Mind and Truth of Manner. (5:23-26.) The spiritual lesson there is the difference between reality and sincerity. The thing that Jesus alters is the temper of our minds, so that we are no longer in bondage to rules and regulations, but find when the difficulties come that we obey our Lord's rules easily. (See Matt. 11:28-30.)

The illustration is of a man in the old Jewish order going to take a paschal lamb to the priest to be slain, and, remembering he had leaven in his house, he had to go back and take the leaven out before he took his offering. Jesus applies it spiritually. If you are going to the altar and you remember someone has something against you, first go and put that right, and if you are a saint, you will find you have the power to do it. A disciple of Jesus has no difficulty in doing what, to worldly people, would be an impossible humiliation. Many of us have sincere manners toward one another, but the test Jesus gives is not the truth of your manner, but the temper of your mind. When you come to the altar, you have something brought to your memory—Jesus does not say when you "rake up something," that is where Satan gets hold of embryo Christians and makes them hyper-conscientious. Jesus says if at the altar there you remember, the inference is that the Spirit of God brings it to your memory, and when He does, never check it. Say, "Yes, Lord, I recognize it," and obey Him at once, no matter what the humiliation is. That is impossible in a worldly person and impossible in you and me till God has altered us. Suppose I do remember something at the altar, and I was in the right and they were in the wrong, and the Spirit of God says to me, "You go and obey;" if I have not had the temper of my mind altered by Jesus, I will say instantly, "No, indeed, do you think I am going to tell them, when I was in the right, that I have to make it up? Immediately they will say, 'I knew I would make you say you were sorry!' " That is the temper of mind in all of us till we have been altered. Immediately we are altered the other temper of mind is there and, to our astonishment, we find we do things we never could do before. Jesus Christ brings men to the practical test, it is not that I say I am pure in heart, it is that I prove I am in my deeds, that the attitude is right, that I am not only sincere in my manner and talk, but I am sincere in the attitude of my mind.

One of the points we do not realize sufficiently is the influence of what we think over what we say. We may say wonderfully truthful things, but what we think is the thing that tells. It is quite possible to say truthful things in a truthful manner, and tell a lie all the time by thinking. I can repeat exactly what I heard you say to Mr. Somebody-else, word for word, every detail scientifically truthful, and yet I can convey a lie by it because the temper of my mind has been a different one to yours when you said the things.

Jesus says be truthful in manner, and the one thing He is "going for" here is to prove that the disposition must be altered. All through the Sermon on the Mount the same thing comes out. Jesus is dealing on the inside, the old law dealt with the outside. Jesus said you have to exceed that, do all the old law, but do much more, and "the only way you can do the much more is by letting me have my way with you, letting me give you my Spirit, by letting me alter you from the inside, and when you come into the different circumstances and I say to you, 'Do this,' don't remember what you were before I altered you, but remember that everything I tell you to do you can do, and the only knowledge you have that you can do it is that you discover you can, immediately you try. Don't say, 'I cannot do that, I tried it before and could not.'" The whole point of our Lord is, "Obey me, and you will find you have a wealth of power inside."

Instantly you obey, you find the temper of your mind is real. The great thing about Jesus is that He makes us real, not only sincere. Remember, the people who are sincere without being real are not hypocrites nor shams, they are perfectly earnest and honest and desirous of fulfilling all that Jesus wants, but they really cannot do it, the reason being they have not received the Person who makes them real, *viz.*, the Holy Spirit.

(3) Lust and License. (5: 27, 28.) Our Lord teaches here what the apostle Paul re-emphasizes in Romans 6: 12, *viz.*, that sin is not in the mortal flesh, but in the principle that rules

the mortal flesh: "Let not sin therefore reign in your mortal body that ye should obey it in the lusts thereof." The "it" he is referring to is the sin that dwells in your mortal body. Our Lord says by implication that what He alters is the principle of desire in our mortal bodies. "Lust," which means "I must have it at once," is the very nature of sin. Jesus alters that and puts love in its place, which is the opposite of lust. Esau and his mess of pottage are a picture of lust; Jacob serving for Rachel is a picture of love. Our Lord in this illustration puts lust and license on the grossest, vilest ground, but remember, it applies all through, from the very lowest basis of immorality. Our Lord puts it on here right up to the very height of spiritual life. Our Lord says that He alters the mainspring of "I must have it at once," the impatience of desire. Never confine lust to the vile, gross elements only, it goes right through. It is that principle Jesus alters. He does not alter our human nature, that does not need altering; He alters the mainspring, and the great marvel of the salvation of Jesus is that He alters heredity. License means, "I will do what I like and care for nobody." Liberty means, "I have the power to do what is right."

Do you see how we are growing? The disciples were taught to lay their account with purity, purity is too deep down for us to go to, our only exhibition of purity is the purity that was in the heart of our Lord, and that is the purity He implants in us. Now He says that is deeper down than you can go, but you will know whether it is there by the disposition that works in circumstances. You will know whether it is there by the temper of mind you exhibit in trying circumstances, and you will know it is there when you come up against circumstances that would have awakened in you in the previous time lust and self-desire, but now they awaken the opposite. It is not a question of a possibility on the inside, but of a possibility that shows itself in performance. That is the only test there is. "He that *doeth* righteousness is righteous, even as he is righteous." (1 John 3:7.)

(4) Direction of Discipline. (5:29, 30.) If Jesus can alter our disposition, what is the need of discipline? Yet in these verses our Lord puts very stern discipline, to the parting with the right arm and the eye. The reason is this, that our physical cases, *i. e.*, mortal bodies, have been used by the wrong disposition, and when the new disposition is put in, the old physical case is not

taken away, it is left there for us to discipline and make it an obedient servant to the new disposition. When God alters a person by regeneration or sanctification, you will always notice the characteristic is a maimed life to begin with, as Jesus describes here. In 5:48, Jesus describes an absolutely different life, not a maimed life, but a perfect life, but in the beginning it is maimed, meaning by that there are a hundred and one things you dare not do and you do not want to do when you are introduced to the new disposition, things that are to you and also in the eyes of the world that knew you, as your right arm and your eye, and the worldly person comes to you and says, "What an absurd idea! Whatever is there wrong in that? What can be wrong in a 'right arm'? It is the best thing you have; how absurd you are, why do you want to go to the extreme swing of the pendulum?" God will make you go to the extreme swing of the pendulum at the beginning. There never was a saint yet who did not have to start with Jesus a maimed life. Jesus says it is better that you should enter into this life, this Christian life, maimed, lovely in God's sight and lame in man's, than that you should be lovely in man's sight and lame in God's. You will find that principle runs all through, and at the beginning Jesus Christ, by His Spirit in you, has to check your doing a great many things that are perfectly right for everybody else but you. Paul mentions the same thing when he says, "Now do not use your limitations to criticize someone else." The world calls you a fanatic and a crank, personally I have no respect for a person who has not been a crank or a fanatic, because it is a sure sign that he has never begun to seriously consider life.

Jesus, when He alters our disposition, takes us back to the first beginning of our physical life, and He teaches us to take our body and put it in harmony with the new disposition, and we have to do it in stern discipline and get the body to express the new disposition, and it can only be done as we obey. The idea Jesus conveys here is that the discipline is to cut off a great many things for your own spiritual life's sake. People say, "Well, I don't see any harm in that, why should I not do it?" Immediately a person argues like that, the proof is as strong as it can be that Jesus Christ is not first. If I am only willing to give up wrong things for Jesus Christ, never let me talk about being in love with Him. Anybody will give up wrong things if he knows how to, but will I give up right things for Him?

A Christian is the only person who has the right to give up his *rights*. You will notice the big difference there is between everyone else's idea of purity and the Lord Jesus Christ's. Our idea of purity, where it does not come from Jesus Christ, is that of according obedience to certain laws and orders; that is not purity, that is apt to be prudery. Read the bald, shocking statements of the Bible, there is nothing prudish about the Bible. The Bible insists on purity, not prudery; that is, you are capable of facing the vilest scenes in life, unspotted. That is what Jesus Christ wants. If He can only make us prudish, why, we would be horrified if we had to go and work for Him in the slums and in the moral abominations in heathendom, we would be shocked all to pieces; but with Jesus Christ's purity, He can take us where He went Himself—in the face of the vilest moral corruptions, the most hideous diseases—and keep us as pure as He kept Himself. The purity Jesus Christ teaches is the purity of His own heart which He puts into you and me. It is always a bad sign when a skeptic says, "There are things in the Bible I would not allow my daughter to read." What is that the evidence of? A vilely impure heart, that is all. The Bible, from cover to cover, will do nothing in the shape of harm, but only good. It is to the impure in heart that these things are corrupting.

B. THE ACCOUNT WITH PRACTICE. (Matt. 5:31-37.)

Practice means what I am continually doing that no one sees or knows but myself.

(1) Scandal. (5:31, 32.) Our Lord taught, by example and precept, that no man should stand up for his own honor, but only for the honor of another. You can easily see in a hundred ways how it worked in the life of our Lord. They called Him a glutton, a winebibber, devil-possessed, a sinner, a madman, and He never opened His mouth; but immediately they said a word against His Father, He not only opened His mouth, but He said some of the most terrible things the world ever heard. Jesus teaches us that by His Spirit He alters the standard of honor in the disciples. Jesus made Himself of no reputation, and the disciples don't bother their heads about what people say about them, but they do bother themselves tremendously about what people think of Jesus Christ. The disciple realizes that his Lord's honor is at stake in his life, not his own honor. The more you meditate on that principle, the more opposed you

find it is to the principle of the world, even the Christian world. The best illustration for scandal is that of mud on your clothes. If you try and touch it while it is wet, you will rub it into the texture, but if you leave it till it is dry, you can flick it and it is gone without a trace. Leave scandal alone, never touch it.

(2) Irreverent Reverence. (5: 33-36.) In our Lord's day the habit of backing up ordinary assertions with an appeal to the name of God was as bad, if not worse, than in our own day. It is not the question of an oath in a law court, Paul took the oath, our Lord said something very like it before Caiaphas. Nowadays we talk most irreverently about the most reverent things. Many of us speak glibly and familiarly about the Holy Ghost, about Jesus and about God. Irreverent reverence, that is what our Lord checks. Do not flippantly talk about those things and those terms which ought to be mentioned with the greatest reverence. I remember an Indian zenana woman who got saved, she could not say many words of English, but I will never forget the way she said the words "Jesus Christ"! She was a very ugly woman, but at the pronouncement of those words her face became transfigured; the whole soul of the woman was in reverent adoration for the

Lord Jesus Christ. Jesus here checks us and says, "Never you call anything in the nature of God or the Holy Ghost to attest what you are saying, speak simply and humbly, realizing that truth in a man is the same as truth in God," and to call in God as a witness to back up what I say is nearly always a sign that what I am saying is not true. If you submit children for a long while to a skeptical atmosphere and call in question all they say, it is that, that first of all instils the habit of swearing. I do not mean using profane language, but it makes children say, "Well, ask him." Such a thought never occurs to a child naturally, it only occurs when the child has to talk to suspicious people, who are continually saying, "Now I do not know whether that is true," and the child gets the idea that it cannot speak the truth unless some one else backs it up. Many of us are responsible for making people call in another witness which they have no right to do.

(3) Integrity. (5:37.) Integrity means the unimpaired state of a thing. Suspicion is of the devil, and is the greatest cause for making people say more than they need to. In that aspect it "cometh of evil." In the other aspect, when I know of eight or ten reasons for the truth of

what I am saying, it is a proof that what I am saying is not strictly true. If it were, we would never have to think of the reasons. Our Lord gets us back to the one simple point, "If I have altered your disposition you will talk like I do; let people do anything they like with your truth, but never explain it." There is a great difference between Jesus Christ and those of us who are His modern followers. Jesus never explained anything, we are always explaining, we are always saying, "Well, I do not mean that, I mean something else." We get into tangles by not leaving the thing alone. If people have made mistakes, leave them alone, let mistakes correct themselves. Our Lord never told His disciples when they made mistakes. They made any number of blunders about Him, but He went quietly on planting the truth. It comes out also with regard to the question of praise. I always like to find out what people think of what I have done when I am not sure of having done well, but when I am certain I have done well, I don't care an atom whether folks praise or not. We have to live on the line of integrity. We find the same thing with regard to fear and courage. We all know the kind of men who say they are not afraid, but the very fact that they say it proves they are.

Jesus Christ puts in a truthfulness that never takes knowledge of itself. It never occurs to a pure, honest heart to back up what it says. It is a wounding insult to be met by suspicion; that is why from the very first we ought never to submit children to suspicion; if we do, we find what Jesus said, that what is more than simple, direct talk comes from the evil one, either in you or in any other person, is true.

C. ACCOUNT WITH PERSECUTION. (Matt. 5:38-42.)

(1) Insult. (5:38, 39.) The picture given in 5:38, 39 is not very familiar to us. In the East a slap on the cheek is the grossest form of insult, its only equivalent with us is spitting in the face. Epictetus, a Roman slave, said a slave would rather be thrashed to death than flicked on the cheek. Jesus says, "Now if you are flicked on the cheek as my representatives, pay no attention," that is, show a disposition that is equivalent to turning the other cheek, which will paralyze them with amazement. Personal insult will be the occasion in the saint of revealing the incredible sweetness of the Lord Jesus Christ.

(2) Extortion. (5:40.) Another picture that is unfamiliar to us. According to the Jew-

ish law, and the law of other countries in our Lord's day, if a man's cloak and coat were taken from him as the result of a lawsuit, he could get back the loan of his cloak to sleep in. Jesus taught His disciples that, "If people extort things from you when you are in my service, let them have the things, but go on with your work."

(3) Tyranny. (5:41, 42.) Under the Roman dominance, the Roman soldiers could compel anyone to be a baggage carrier for a mile. (Simon, the Cyrenian, is a case in point; the Roman soldiers compelled him to be baggage carrier for Jesus.) Jesus says, "If you are my disciple, you will always do more than your duty, you will go the second mile." There will be none of the spirit of, "Oh, well, I cannot do any more, they have always misrepresented and misunderstood me." Jesus says if you are His disciple, you will always do more than your duty. It would have been a sad outlook for us if He had not gone the second mile.

Verse 42 is the most radical of all. The fact that modern Christians wiggle, twist, compromise about this verse springs from infidelity in the ruling providence of our Heavenly Father. Modern people say, "It is absurd. Do you mean to tell me I have to give to everyone that asks?

if I do, every beggar in the place will be at my door." Will they? Try it. I have yet to find a person who has fulfilled Jesus Christ's command who did not find that God restrained the people who beg. You will find at the very heart of that modern wiggle is infidelity—"I do not believe God can control the beggars; if once I am known to give to everybody that asks, then they will come." Try it. I tell you they will not. If ever God's ruling is seen, it is seen when once a disciple obeys what Jesus Christ says.

Another thing, Jesus Christ never taught this: give because they deserve it; He says, "Give because I tell you." You can always find a hundred and one reasons why you should not obey our Lord's statements, the reason being that we are always more apt to trust reasonings than reason, and reasonings always mean we do not take God into calculation at all. "Does this man deserve what I am giving him?" Why, immediately you say that before Jesus Christ, the Spirit of God says to you, "Who are you? Do you deserve all you have? Do you deserve the salvation you have? Do you deserve all the blessings I have given you more than the other man?" The great motive of all giving is Jesus Christ's command. Tolstoi applied the principles of Jesus without the

Spirit of Jesus; he applied the statements of Jesus literally, but he absolutely disbelieved in being born again, consequently there was no restraining hand of God, no proof that God was with him or in him in those particulars. But once let a disciple get rightly related to Jesus Christ, and let the Spirit of God alter the disposition, then as circumstances arise obey His principles, and you will find exactly what Jesus teaches: "God is your Father, He loves you, you will never think of anything He will forget, therefore you have no business to worry."

Study Number Four

A. DIVINE RULE OF LIFE.

1. Exhortation.
   Matthew 5:45-47.
2. Example.
   Matthew 5: 46.
3. Expression.
   Matthew 5: 48.

B. DIVINE REGION OF RELIGION.

1. Philanthropy.
   Matthew 6: 1-4.
2. Prayer.
   Matthew 6: 5-14.
3. Penance.
   Matthew 5:16-18.

C. DIVINE REASONINGS OF MIND.

1. Doctrine of Deposit.
   Matthew 6: 19-21.
2. Doctrine of Division.
   Matthew 6: 22, 23.
3. Doctrine of Detachment.
   Matthew 6: 24.

D. DIVINE REASONINGS OF FAITH.

1. Careful Carelessness.
   Matthew 6: 25.
2. Careless Unreasonableness.
   Matthew 6: 26.
3. Careful Uselessness.
   Matthew 6: 27-29.
4. Careful Infidelity.
   Matthew 6: 30-32.
5. Concentrated Consecration.
   Matthew 6: 33, 34.

STUDY NUMBER FOUR

MATTHEW 5 AND 6

A. DIVINE RULE OF LIFE. (Matt. 5:45-47.)

Our Lord concludes by a divine rule which we by His Spirit ought to apply to every circumstance and condition of our lives. Our Lord does not make statements which we have to follow literally; if He did, we would not grow in grace. He gives us a principle and a rule of conduct, and we have to rely upon His Spirit to teach us to apply them to the various circumstances in which we find ourselves.

(1) Exhortation. (5:45-47.) Our Lord's exhortation here is to be generous in our behavior to all men, whether they be good or bad. The marvel of the divine love is that God exhibits His love to bad people whom we desert. For instance, in Luke 15, we can understand after a bit how God is represented as the Father loving the prodigal son, but He also exhibits His love to

the elder brother, to whom we feel a strong antipathy. Beware of walking in the spiritual life according to our natural affinities. We all have natural affinities which we bring with us to the world, that is, people we like and others we do not like, some people we get on well with and others we do not. Never let those likes and dislikes be the rule of your Christian life. God says through John, "Walk in the light as He is in the light," and God gives you communion with people you have no natural affinities for.

(2) Example. (5:46.) Woven into the words of our Lord's exhortation is His reference to our Example, and our Example is not a good man, or even a good Christian, but God Himself. (See 5:45 and 48.) I do not think we allow the big surprise of that to lay hold of us. Jesus never says anywhere, "Follow the best example you know, follow good Christians you know, watch the people who love me and follow them." He says, "Follow your Father which is in Heaven."

(3) Expression. (5:48.) The expression of Christian character is not good doing, but God-likeness. In verse 48 there is a re-emphasis of verse 20. The *perfection* of verse 48 refers to the disposition and temper of God in us. The

Revised Version reads, "Ye shall be perfect," but that does not mean in a future state, it means, "You shall be perfect if you let me work in you what I have been describing." The whole point is, if the Spirit of God has transformed you on the inside, you will exhibit not good human characteristics, but good divine characteristics in a human heing. In verse 48 our Lord completes the picture He began to give in verses 29, 30. In the former He pictures a maimed life; here He pictures a well-balanced life, for holiness means a perfect balance between my disposition and the laws of God. In verses 29, 30 our Lord pictures the maimed life, which is the characteristic of everyone of us at the beginning, and if we have never had that characteristic, the question is very open whether we have received the Spirit of God, because if the Spirit of God has regenerated us He makes us take the opposite extreme to everything we have been doing. He makes us what people call "fanatics." So you very often find in our own case and in others that, if we are to obey the Spirit of God, we have to live a limited and maimed life. But in verse 48 Jesus gives the picture of a perfectly full-orbed life, not hereafter, but here. It is only as we walk in the light as He is in the light, that we begin to understand the example Jesus gives us—God, not men. It is not sufficient to be good, to do the right thing; you must have your goodness stamped by the image and superscription of Jesus. It is supernatural all through. The whole secret of a Christian, according to Jesus, is the supernatural made natural in us by the grace of God. The way it works out is not in having times of communion with God, but the expression of it works out in the practical details of our life. If we have been regenerated, the proof of it is when we come in contact with the things that create a "buzz." We find, to our great astonishment, we have a power we never had before, a power to keep wonderfully poised in the center of it all, a power that God explains only by the cross of Jesus Christ. It is not a question of putting statements of our Lord's in front of us and trying to live up to them, it is receiving His Spirit and finding we can live up to them with little effort.

B. DIVINE REGION OF RELIGION. (Matt. 6: 1-18.)

The region of religion means the domain of my life lifted to God before men; the other region of our natural life lived to men before God. In

Matthew 5 our Lord demands that our dispositions be all right in our ordinary calling before Him. Now He says you have to live to me before men. The main idea in the region of religion is, "Your eye on Me, not on men."

(1) Philanthropy. (6: 1-4.) This corresponds to verse 42 of chapter 5, with this difference, that Matthew 5: 42 refers to the life lived with the eye on God. Briefly summed up, it means this: "Have no other motive in giving than to please God." Our Lord allows of no other motive, but you find when you look at modern philanthropy it has every other motive but that. The motive we are continually being *egged* on with, is, "It will do them good, they need the help, they deserve it." Jesus never brings that aspect out in the whole of His Sermon. In chapter 5 it is, "Give because I tell you," and here it is, "Don't have mixed motives." Our Lord is picturing in chapter 6 something the Jews were familiar with. The Jews used to put their money in the boxes in the woman's court of the Temple, and the Pharisees put their money in with a great clang which sounded like a trumpet. Jesus was standing in the Temple and heard the clanging sound of the gifts of the Pharisees, and He said, "Now don't do that sort of thing, their motive is to be known

as generous givers; if you are my disciples, never give with any other motive than that you are pleasing God." It is a very penetrating thing to ask yourself this question before God, What was my motive in doing that kind act? You will be astounded how rarely the Spirit of God gets a chance to fit our motives on to be right with God, we mix them with a thousand and one other motives, which Jesus steadily makes simple, one motive only, "your eye on me." That is the way we become children of God.

(2) Prayer. (6: 5-14.) Prayer here is looked at in the same way as philanthropy, with the one motive, *viz.*, to please God. "Your Father knoweth what things ye have need of before ye ask Him." (Verse 8.) Then common sense says, "Why ask Him?" Because the whole idea of prayer in this chapter is that Jesus is saying, "Watch your motive before God, have no other motive as Christians than to know your Heavenly Father." Notice all through this chapter the essential simplicity of our Lord's main principle—right towards God, right towards God, no matter what people think.

(3) Penance. (6: 16-18.) Penance is putting myself into a physical strait-jacket for the sake of disciplining my spiritual character. Pen-

ance is the great note in the Roman Catholic religion, and it is altogether omitted in Protestantism, and we have been the losers in the consequence. We have been so full of antipathy to Roman Catholic doctrines that we have missed altogether what our Lord and also St. Paul said about the need to have penance. You will find that physical sloth will upset spiritual devotion quicker than anything. If the devil can't get at us by enticing to sin, he gets in by "sleeping-sickness," spiritually. "Now you can't possibly get up in the morning to pray, you are working hard all day, and you can't give that time to prayer, you must not do this and that, God doesn't expect it." Jesus says, "God does expect it."

In verse 16 our Lord says when you do fast don't make cheap martyrs of yourself, pretend by a joyful face that you are not putting yourself through the stern discipline that God knows you are. The pictures were familiar to Jews, they were commanded to pray several times a day, and the Pharisees took care that they happened to be in the midst of a city when the hour for prayer came, and they would jump down, and in an ostentatious manner give themselves to prayer in public. Jesus says, "Don't be like that. That is their motive, they want to be known as praying people and verily they have their reward." And the same with their times of fasting, they looked so sad and miserable that everyone knew they were fasting. Jesus says when you have to go through a period of discipline before God, pretend you are not going through it. (Verse 17.) If ever I can tell to others the discipline I put myself through in order to further my life with God, the discipline from that moment becomes useless. Our Lord repeats over and over again, You have to have a relationship between you and God which nobody knows and nobody dare know; you must have something between you and God that the dearest friend on earth never guesses; if you have a life of discipline with God, don't say a word about it, appear not unto men to fast. The Spirit of God will apply it to each of us, and we will see there are lines of discipline, lines of limitation, physical and mental, which the Spirit of God says, "Now you must not allow yourself." When you fast, fast to your Father in secret, not before men. The ostensible fasts on the outside are of no use; it is the fasts on the inside that God knows.

C. DIVINE REASONINGS OF MIND. Matt. 6: 19-24.)

We mean by divine reasonings, the way a

Christian thinks about everything. Until this is learned by our obedience to God, the majority of us drift in Christian experience without any thinking. One of the most fruitful things is to find out what the New Testament says about the mind. The Spirit of God comes through Paul and Peter and John with the one steady appeal to stir up our minds. The only way Satan can get in as an angel of light is to those Christians whose hearts are right, but whose minds are not stirred up. Our Lord here deals with the question of the mind, how I am to think and reason about things.

(1) Doctrine of Deposit. (6: 19-21.) In thinking as a Christian, every effort to persuade myself that the real treasure of my heart and mind is with God is a sure sign that it is not. If I have to reason with myself, and say I am perfectly certain that my treasure is in Heaven, and my motives are right with God, then you may be sure it is not so. The first thing Jesus says is, "Lay up for yourselves treasures in Heaven." Spiritual experience means that the Spirit of God in our hearts teaches us to fasten our eyes and our thinking on God, and when in practical life we come to deal with money matters and matters of earth, the Spirit of God reminds us, to our

great peace and delight, that our treasures are in Heaven, and we find we begin to do the right thing with our property and money and everything that has to do with this earth in a way that astonishes us. The ideal is not to make out that my motive is right, but that the motive has been put right, and therefore it begins to put my thinking right. All the confusion and conflict arises when people try to be Christians without the Spirit of God; they try to reason it out. The first thing we have to do is to be born again of the Spirit of God, and obey Him as He begins to explain to our mind that the real motive at the heart of it is all right.

(2) Doctrine of Division. (6:22, 23.) We have to learn from this that the correct understanding of all physical and mental things is by a single eye. That is the symbol for the conscience of a man being put right with God by the Holy Spirit. One idea runs all through our Lord's teaching: "Right with God, right with God!" First, second and third! The proof that we are right with God is that we never try to be right, because the Spirit of God has put us in the right relationship. That is a roundabout way of saying that if I have been born again of the Holy Ghost, I am right with God, then if

I keep in the light as He is in the light, that keeps my eye single, and slowly and surely all my bodily actions begin to be put into the right relationship, and everything becomes full of harmony and simplicity and peace. To rightly divide material matters and interests, a man must be born from above.

(3) Doctrine of Detachment. (6:24.) This is a fundamental and favorite theme of our Lord's: you cannot be good and bad at one and the same time, and you cannot serve God with an eye on successful service; and you can never make "honesty the best policy," a motive. These thoughts run all through Jesus Christ's teaching. If I am to be holy, there is one consideration, I have to stand right with God, and see that that relationship is the one thing that is never dimmed in my practical life, and all other things will right themselves. Jesus says you cannot serve God and mammon. What we mean by a worldly Christian is one who frankly disbelieves that statement of our Lord's, and says, "Oh, yes, with a little more skill and subtlety and wisdom (we call it diplomacy), a little more compromise, we can serve both." The devil's temptation to our Lord to compromise is repeated over and over again. The doctrine of detachment means that

I must realize that a division is made between the Christian and the world, as high as Heaven and as deep as Hell. That is the reason Jesus says, as He did in chapter 5 (also in 1 Peter 4:4), that when you get right with God you become what the world calls "a fanatic." When you get right with God you become something that is contemptible in the eyes of the world. Try to put into practice any of the principles of the Sermon on the Mount and you will be treated, not with indignation, but with amusement, and if you persist in it you will find the world gets annoyed and detests you. In the beginning of the Christian life always make allowance for the swing of the pendulum. It is not an accident, it is the set purpose of God that we go to the extreme reaction from what we were before. He sees that we do the exact opposite of all we did before, God does not gradually overcome it, He violently breaks us from it, and only brings us back into the domain of men when we are perfectly right with Him, so when we get back into the domain of men we are among them, yet not of them. (John 17.) When we are matured in godliness and have proved to Jesus that we do not compromise between mammon and godliness, then He trusts us and trusts His own honor in placing us where the world, the flesh and the devil may try us, knowing that "He that is in us is greater than he that is in the world."

D. DIVINE REASONINGS OF FAITH. (Matt. 6: 25-34.)

The reasonings of faith mean the practical working out in my life of my implicit, determined confidence in God.

(1) Careful Carelessness. (6: 25.) Jesus does not say that a man who doesn't think about anything is blessed; that man is a fool. Jesus says you must be carefully careless about everything but one thing: "Your right relationship to me." Our Lord teaches here the complete reversal of the reasonings of a practical, sensible person who has no faith in God whatever. Our Lord tells the disciples that they have to be studiously careful that they are careless about how they stand to self-interest, to food, to drink and to personal property, because they are set on minding the right relationship to God. I have to be carefully careless for one reason. Ever so many people are careless over what they eat and drink, and they suffer for it; they are careless about what they put on, and they look as they have no business to look; they are careless about

property, and God will hold them responsible for it. What Jesus is saying is that the great care of the life is to make the relationship to God the one care, and everything else secondary. Immediately you look at that you find it is the most revolutionary statement human ears ever listened to. You will find our arguing is exactly the opposite, even the most spiritual of us. We say, "I must live, I must make so much money, I must be clothed, I must be fed," that is how it begins; that is, the great concern of the life is not God; the great concern of the life is how I am going to fit myself to live. Jesus says, "Reverse the order, get rightly related to Me first, see that you maintain that as the greatest care of your life, never put the concentration of your care on the other things." You will find, if you read the Old and New Testaments, the reason God allows "dry rot," bankruptcy, disease and upset, is that His children will not obey Jesus Christ on that line. It is one of the severest disciplines, to allow the Spirit of God to bring us into harmony with Jesus on these concluding verses of Matthew 6.

(2) Careful Unreasonableness. (6: 26.) To be careful of all that the natural man says we must be careful over, Jesus declares unreasonable, because the natural man says to think about

the means of living in order to live. Picture to yourself all the sparrows and blackbirds and thrushes sitting on hedges in the early spring, thinking and worrying their heads about how they would stick their feathers in. Jesus says they don't bother themselves at all. The very thing that makes them what they are is not their thought, but the Father's which is in Heaven. Jesus says, "You maintain obedience to the Holy Spirit, who is the real principle of your life, and He will supply the feathers for you. You are much better than a sparrow." Our Lord uses that illustration more than once. He does not use it by accident, He uses it purposely to show us the utter unreasonableness, from His standpoint, of being so anxious about the means of living.

(3) Careful Uselessness. (6:27-29.) Our Lord says that it is utterly useless to mistake careful consideration of circumstances for that which produces character. "Consider the lily," it obeys the law of its life in the circumstances it is placed in. As Christians, consider your hidden life with God, *i. e.*, pay attention to the source, and God will look after the outflow. The hardest working thing is a bird, but it does not work to stick feathers on itself; it obeys the law of its life and

becomes what it is. Jesus Christ's argument is, "You are the men and women who are the fittest to do the work of the world, the other people are not, because the other people have the ulterior motive of looking after circumstances in order to produce a fine character. It cannot be done. If you will concentrate on the life I give you, make that your business, you are perfectly free for all the other things because you know your Father is watching the life on the inside." You cannot produce the life on the inside by heeding the outside all the time. Imagine a lily doing what some of us want to do spiritually. "Oh, I must give up this, I must go here and there"—quick-silver Christians. Imagine a lily hauling itself out of a pot and saying, "Well, I don't think I smell nice here, I don't think I look exactly right." The lily's duty is to do what it does—obey the law of its life where it is placed by the gardener. Paul says, "All these things work together for your good." Watch your life with God, see that that is right and you will grow all right.

(4) Careful Infidelity. (6:30-32.) Jesus tersely sums up common-sense carefulness, if it is in a person without the indwelling Spirit of God, as infidelity. Since you received the Spirit

of God and obeyed Him, whenever you try to put other things first, you find confusion, you find the Spirit of God presses through and says, "No, this first, where do I come in this new relationship, in this mapped-out holiday, in these new books you are buying?" The Spirit of God always presses that point till we learn to obey the first consideration; knowing that God is my Father, He loves me, I shall never think of anything He will forget; why should I worry? It is not only wrong to worry, it is real infidelity, because it means, "God cannot look after my practical little details" (and it is never anything else that worries us). Did you ever notice what Jesus says (in Matthew 13) will choke the life He puts in? The devil? No, "The cares of this world." It is the little foxes, the little worries, always, and that is how infidelity begins. The great cure for infidelity is obedience to the Spirit of God. If once we get into our hearts and lives in thinking, what God has put in us spiritually, we would find that the men and women who are rightly related to God are the men and women who carry in them heaven on the way to Heaven, that is, they are free to do the work of the world like no one else. A business man with the Spirit of God in him can do the work of a business man ten thousand-fold better than a man without the Spirit, because the responsibility of his life is off him and on God.

(5) Concentrated Consecration. (6: 33, 34.) Our Lord teaches that the one great secret of Christian health and prosperity is concentration on God and His purposes.

Study Number Five

MATTHEW SEVEN.

A. CHRISTIAN CHARACTERISTICS.

1. The Uncritical Temper.
   Matthew 7:1.
2. The Undeviating Test.
   Matthew 7:2.
3. The Undesirable Truth-Teller.
   Matthew 7:3-5.

B. CHRISTIAN CONSIDERATENESS.

1. The Need to Discriminate.
   Matthew 7:6.
2. The Notion of Divine Control.
   Matthew 7:10.
3. The Necessity for Discernment.
   Matthew 7:11.

C. CHRISTIAN COMPREHENSIVENESS.

1. The Positive Margin of Righteousness.
2. The Proverbial Maxim of Reasonableness.
3. The Principal Meaning of Revelation.

STUDY NUMBER FIVE

MATTHEW 7.

A. CHRISTIAN CHARACTERISTICS. (Matt. 7: 1-5.)

A characteristic is something which steadily prevails, not something that occasionally manifests itself. It is what people do steadily and persistently that makes their character. This chapter indicates the steady characteristics of a Christian, not what a Christian is occasionally; that is a spasmodic thing which God mourns over, "Thy goodness is as a morning cloud," He says.

(1) The Uncritical Temper. (7: 1.) Our Lord says regarding critical judgment, "Abstain!" This sounds very strange, because the characteristic of the Holy Spirit in a believer is to reveal to him the things that are wrong; but the strangeness is only on the surface, the discernment of the Holy Spirit is not for purposes of criticism, but for purposes of conversion. The

Holy Spirit reveals to you something of the nature of unbelief and sin perhaps in other people, perhaps in yourself. His purpose is not to make you feel the smug satisfaction of a critical spectator, "Well, thank God I am not like that," but exactly the opposite, to make you turn clean round from the whole thing, or, if it is in someone else, to make you lay hold of God so that God enables him to turn away from the wrong thing. (See I John 5: 16.) Criticism is not possible to a wholesome spiritual life, for when criticism becomes a habit it destroys moral energy, kills faith, and paralyzes spiritual force. The critical faculty is an intellectual one, not a moral one. A critic must be removed from what he criticizes. The only person who can criticize human life is the Holy Ghost. No human being dare criticize another human being, because immediately he does, he puts himself in a different place altogether to the one he criticizes. Our Lord al'ows no room for criticism; He makes any amount of room for discrimination. When a man criticizes a work of art or a piece of music his information must be complete, and he stands away from the thing he criticizes, and is able to criticize it as superior to it. Jesus says you can never take that attitude, and if anyone does take that spirit of criticism he grieves the Spirit of God and instantly puts himself in the wrong position. Criticism when it decomposes becomes deadly. If you are criticized much, it has the effect of decomposing you, you become good for nothing. After a good dose of criticism all the gumption and power and spiritual life is knocked out of you for a time. That is never the work of the Holy Ghost and never the work of the saint; it is the work of the devil always. Whenever criticism is used, it is Jesus saying, "Apply that to yourself," but never apply it to anyone else. Any point of view that makes me decompose other persons, makes me lynx-eyed to see where they are wrong, and the effect of my seeing where they are wrong is to paralyze them; it does not do them any good, which shows that criticism never came from the Holy Ghost. If I come and say, "Well, I love you, but I must tell you so and so," I simply am an unreal fraud, I do not love you, I have put myself into a position far superior to you, I am in the position of a critic of a work of art; but Jesus says a disciple can never stand off from another life and criticize it. So He advocates here to be of an uncritical spirit. Let that maxim of the Lord's sink into your heart and you will see how it hauls you up, "Judge not;" why, we are always at it. Any power in me that separates the set of powers in another soul and prevents it from being one force is critical and bad.

The effect of criticism is always to divide the powers of the other person. You know some simple, honest soul who is doing things you know to be wrong, now be careful, if you take the part of the devil and become a critic, you will divide the powers of that soul and prevent it being a force for anything. You will knock it all to pieces. Take Jesus Christ's way, tell Him, and "I will give you life for him that sins not unto death." You will find when the Holy Ghost discriminates, He criticizes in the true position of a critic, that is, He is able to show what is wrong without wounding and hurting; when we criticize we wound in such a way that the powers never get back to their right purposes. Jesus says to be uncritical in your temper. It is not done once and for all, we have to be always remembering that that is our Lord's rule of conduct. Beware of anything that puts you in the superior person's place.

(2) The Undeviating Test. (7: 2.) That verse is not a haphazard guess, it is an eternal law of God. A scriptural case in point: when Mary of Bethany broke the alabaster box of oint-

ment, the disciples said, "What a waste." John says that one disciple in particular said the words, *viz.*, Judas. When Jesus referred to Judas in John 17, He called him a "son of waste." Whatever judgment I give, it is measured to me again. "I am perfectly certain Mrs. So-and-so has been criticizing me." Well, what have you been doing? You will never find it fail, and Jesus puts it here in connection with criticism, if you have been shrewd in finding out defects in others, remember that will be exactly the measure given to you, that is the way people will judge you, and in Psalm 18 the Psalmist says that is how God is to us, if we are "froward" to God, He is "froward" to us; if we are pure towards God, He is pure towards us. It works from God's throne right down; life serves back in the coin you pay.

Romans 2:1 applies it in a still more definite way, and says that the person who criticizes another is guilty of that very thing, not only in possibility but in actuality. We do not believe the statements of the Bible to begin with, for instance, do we believe that statement that what I criticize in another I am guilty of myself? God does not look at the act, He looks at the possibility. The consequence is this, we can always tell sin in another, why? Because we are sinners and the great danger is mistaking carnal suspicion for the conviction of the Holy Ghost. The fact that I can see hypocrisy and fraud and unreality in other people is because they are all in my heart, and if I put myself in a superior position and tell them of it, I have put myself in the place of the Holy Ghost. Take that idea and see what Jesus says, "Out of the human heart proceed," and then follows the catalogue. When the Holy Ghost convicts He convicts for conversion, that they might turn round and be put in another place and have different characteristics. The great characteristic of a saint is humility, that is, feeling the full realization of, "Yes, all those things and all the other evils would have been manifested in me but for the grace of God, therefore I have no right to judge." Jesus says, "Don't," for if you do, it will be measured to you exactly as you have judged. Which one of us would dare stand before God and say, "My God, judge me as I have judged my fellowmen?" We have judged our fellowmen as sinners; if God judged us like that, we would go to Hell. God judges us through the marvelous atonement of Jesus Christ.

(3) The Undesirable Truth-teller. The kind impudence of the average truth-teller is in-

spired of the devil when it comes to pointing out the defects of other people. Watch, for instance, the characteristics of the devil in the Bible. The devil is lynx-eyed for things he can criticize, and we have all had part and parcel with him in times past; we have all been shrewd. "I just want to tell you, my friend, you have something in your eye that is very objectionable, let me take it out and you will feel better;" that puts me in a superior position to you. I am further on than you, a finer spiritual character. Where do you get that characteristic? In the Lord Jesus Christ? Never, He took on Himself the form of a servant,—"I speak the words my Father would have me speak." How did He do it? By submitting His intellect to His Father, and when the Spirit of God works through His saints He works through them unbeknown to them; He works through them like light; He concentrates His light on them, and you know what is wrong with you, and if you do not understand the principle, you will say, "That person is always criticizing me." He is nothing of the sort; it is the Spirit of God through him that has discerned in you what is wrong. But what Jesus is pointing out is, "Beware of taking the place of the Holy Spirit; beware of putting yourself in the superior person's place."

The last curse in a Christian's life is the other person who becomes a providence to you, quite certain you cannot do anything without him, and if you do not heed him it will be very bad for you and very risky. The position is one Jesus has ridiculed here with terrific power. He actually says in verse 5, "Thou hypocrite." The word hypocrite does not mean a person who is playing two parts consciously for his own ends; the word hypocrite is literally, play-actor, one whose reality is not in keeping with sincerity. When we begin to find fault with other people, we are not hypocrites; we are perfectly sincere, and say, "All I desire is their good," but Jesus says in reality you are a fraud; you are a play-actor. "Thou hypocrite, first cast out the beam out of thine own eye, and then shalt thou see clearly to cast out the mote out of thy brother's eye." If I have let God remove the beam from my own outlook on life by His mighty grace, I will carry with me the sunlight confidence and hope that God can easily do for my brother what He has done for me, because he only has a splinter; I have had a log of wood! Look for a moment in your own heart and you find this is the confidence God's salvation gives you, "I am so amazed that God has altered me that I can despair of nobody." When anyone comes across you after you have been marvelously saved by the grace of God, you have the sunshine confidence that inspires him, and you say, "Oh, yes, God can undertake for you; you are only a little bit wrong, but I was wrong down to the remote attitude of my mind; I was a mean, prejudiced, self-interested, self-seeking person, and God altered me, and therefore I can never despair of you." Beware of the unconscious twist that makes you feel like pious Christians, who can talk well; but by laying to heart these sturdy rules of our Lord's, let us grow up into Him in all things. Reflect on the first five verses of this chapter, and you will see at once why a man like Daniel had to bow his head in vicarious humiliation and intercession. "I have sinned," he said, "with Thy people," and the call every now and again comes to communities and nations as it came to Daniel. These statements of Jesus save us from that fearful peril of spiritual conceit, "Thank God, I am not as other men."

B. CHRISTIAN CONSIDERATENESS. (7: 7-11.)

Consider how God dealt and deals with you, says our Lord, and then consider again that you do likewise to others. "Never believe that thing that ought not to be true."

(1) The Need to Discriminate. (7:6.) In this verse Jesus inculcates the need to carefully examine what you present in the way of God's truth to other people. If you present, He says, the perils of God's revelation to unspiritual people, they will trample the pearls under foot and turn again and make a havoc of you. Jesus does not say they will turn and trample you under their feet; that would not matter so much, but they will trample the truth of God under their feet and rend you. The Holy Spirit alone can teach any one of us what that means. There are some truths of God that God will not make simple, and that is why Jesus said, "I speak in parables." The only thing God makes plain in the Bible is the way of salvation and the way of sanctification; after that it depends entirely on my walking in the light. Over and over people "water down" the Word of God to suit those who are not spiritual, the consequence is the Word of God is trampled under the feet of swine, and the people of God are being rent in pieces. What we have to ask ourselves is, "What way am I flinging God's truth before unspiritual swine?" The words are not

mere human words, they are the words of Jesus Christ.

When Jesus talks about our confession before men, He never says to confess anything but Himself ("He that confesseth *Me* before men"), and you will find every time you give a testimony on another line, what Jesus says here is true, the testimony on other lines is for saints, for those who understand and are spiritual; your testimony to the world is Jesus Christ, confess Him. "He saved me, He sanctified me, He puts me right with God." Jesus says if you do that, "I will glorify you before my Father in Heaven. On the other hand, be careful how you give my holy things to dogs." Dogs are a symbol of the folks who live on the streets, the outside people who say there is nothing mysterious in the Bible, it is not inspired, it is simply an ordinary book; don't cast your holy things before them, and be careful that you don't give the pearl of God's truth to men who are swine. Paul gives illustration after illustration, as our Lord does, of the pearl of sanctification being dragged in the mire of fornication. It all comes through people not revering and not respecting the mighty caution of our Lord Jesus Christ.

(2) The Notion of Divine Control. (7:7-10.) Our Lord, by the simple argument of these verses, urges us to keep our minds filled with the notion of God's control behind everything, and that means that the disciple must always maintain an attitude of perfect trust and an eagerness to continually ask God for things and for answers to questions; those things are not spontaneously given us by the Holy Spirit. Paul makes a big distinction between being possessed of the Spirit and forming the mind of Christ. Jesus is laying down rules for conduct of those who have the Spirit. *Notion* your mind with the idea that God is there. If once all the mind is notioned along that line, when you are in difficulties it is as easy as breathing to remember, "Why, my Father knows all about it." It is not an effort, it comes naturally when perplexities are very pressing; before you have gone and asked this and that person, now the notion is forming so powerfully in you that you simply go to God about it. You will always know whether the notion is working by the way you act in difficult circumstances. Who is the first one you go to? What is the first thing you do? What is the first power you rely on? It is the rule that works on the principle we indicated in Matthew 6, God is my

Father, He loves me, I shall never think of anything He'll forget, why should I worry? There are times when God cannot lift the darkness from you, but trust Him; Jesus said He will appear to you like an unkind friend, but He is not; He will appear to you like an unnatural father, but He is not; He will appear to you like an unjust judge, but He is not. Keep that notion strong. If we let these searchlights go straight down to the root of our lives, we shall find why Jesus said, "Don't judge," we won't have any time to; the whole of our time will be taken up living in the life and power of God so that He can pour out through us rivers of living water; some of us are so concerned about the outflow that it dries up. We continually ask, "Am I of any use?" Jesus tells us how we are to be of use: "If you believe on me, out of you will flow rivers of living water." Keep the notion strong and growing, of the mind of God behind all things. Nothing happens in any particular unless God's will is behind; therefore I rest perfectly confident. And remember, prayer is not only asking, it is an attitude, an attitude that produces an atmosphere in which asking is perfectly natural.

(3) The Necessity for Discernment. (7: 11.) The discernment here needed is the reasoning fa-

culty of the saint's mind applied to the saint's self. If you, an evil being, saved by grace, can have such wonderfully kind thoughts and do such wonderfully kind things, how much more will your Heavenly Father give good things to those who ask Him? Probably one of the things that most scares the average evangelical Christian is when he hears some of us saying to an ordinary sinner, "If you ask God for the Holy Spirit, He will give Him you." How shocking! Fancy telling a sinner to ask God to give him the Holy Spirit! They give the old reasoning, "But I thought the Bible said, if I regard iniquity in my heart the Lord will not hear me." Certainly He won't, but that is when you are a Christian; if you are rightly related to God and regard iniquity in your heart, God won't hear your prayer; but Jesus is speaking of the time before that. "If you, being evil."

We put ourselves in God's place, in the place of the superior person; Jesus says, "Get this reasoning incorporated into you. How much have you deserved? Nothing, everything has been given you by God." We find, over and over again, by our actions and sympathy to certain people, we blame God for His neglect of them, and God never says a word; we never say a word against God, but by our attitude we say that we are filling up what God forgot to do. Jesus says. "Never have that notion, never allow it to come in." In all probability the Spirit of God will begin to show that because we have neglected what we ought to have done they are where they are.

Take the great craze of what is called "Socialism," which is getting into the very churches. The Church is saying that Jesus Christ came to be a social reformer. A ridiculous notion. We are to be social reformers, not God. God came to alter us, and we are trying now to shirk our responsibility and put it on God and say God does that; the thing He does is to alter our disposition and put us right. These rules of Jesus would instantly make social reformers, it would begin straight away where we live. What am I like in my relationship to my father and mother, to my brothers and sisters, my friends, my employers, my employees? Have I this habitual spiritual discernment of understanding that all the good things that have been given to me have been given by the sheer sovereign grace of God?

Then God save me from the mean, accursed. economical notion that I must only help the people who deserve it! Sometimes one can almost hear the Spirit of God shout in the heart, "Who are you, that you talk like that? Did you deserve the salvation of God; did you deserve the sanctification that God has given you; did you deserve to be filled with the Spirit?" It is all done out of the sheer sovereign mercy of God. "Then be like your Father in Heaven," says Jesus; "have a perfect disposition like His." Again Jesus puts it, "Love as I have loved." That is not done once and for all; it is a continual, steadfast, growing habit of life.

Humility and holiness always go together. You find, whenever the hardness and the harshness begin to creep into personal actions toward one another, no matter what the preaching is like, the preaching may be as stern and true as God's Word, but if the harshness and hardness come into our actions, we may be certain we are swerving from the light. Never "water down" God's truth, and never forget when we deal with one another that we are sinners saved by grace, no matter where we stand. If we stand in the fulness of the blessing of God, we stand there by no other right than the sheer sovereign grace of God.

C. CHRISTIAN COMPREHENSIVENESS. (7:12.)

Christian grace comprehends all the man. (See Mark 12: 30, 31.) It is not that you will be pure in heart only, not only that you will have a mind enlightened, not only a soul put right, not only divine strength given, but the whole lot comprehended by the marvelous power and grace of God. That is what Jesus is referring to in verse 12—the whole man, body, soul and spirit, being brought into fascinating captivity to the Lord Jesus Christ. An illustration is that of the gas mantel; if it is not rightly adjusted, it does not glow rightly, only one bit glows, but get it adjusted exactly, then when the light comes the whole thing is comprehended in one great blaze of light. That is what Jesus indicates here, that every bit of the nature (not parts of it, some of us have goodness in spots) has to be absolutely absorbing till we are one glow with the comprehensive goodness of God. Paul puts it this way, "If ye are children of light, walk in the light, and ye shall have your fruit in all righteousness, in all goodness and in all truth." (See Eph. 5:8,9.)

(1) The Positive Margin of Righteousness. The limit to the manifested grace of God in me is my body, and the whole of my body. Some of us can understand having a pure heart, having minds rightly adjusted to God, being indwelt by the Spirit, but what about the incandescent body, what about the finger tips,

what about the bodily organs, what about the bodily relationship, what about the eyes and the mouth and the ears? That is the margin of righteousness in me.

You will find that there is a divorce possible in our outlook that is not possible in Jesus Christ. We make a divorce between the clear intellectual understanding of things and the practical outcome. Jesus has nothing to do with it, He won't estimate our fine intellectual conception unless the practical outcome is shown in reality. There is no estimate ever given by our Lord of an eloquent, sincere prophet or preacher. He sums such up in Matthew 7. They were sincere, and were honoring the Word, so the devils were cast out, but Jesus said, "Depart from me."

We have a very great snare in our capacity to understand a thing clearly with our minds and exhaust it by stating it, and you will often find that overmuch earnestness blinds the life to reality. When once you begin to get in earnest, you will find that becomes your god, it is the earnestness and zeal with which things are said and done, and you find after awhile the reality is not there; the real, wonderful power and presence of God are not manifesting themselves through the body; there are relationships at home, or in business, or in private that show when the veneer is taken off, that you are not real. The great thing for us all in this study of the Sermon on the Mount is to allow the principles and rules of Jesus to soak right straight down into our very make-up. It would be like a baptism of light to let these teachings of Jesus soak us through and through until we are incandescent.

(2) The Proverbial Maxim of Reasonableness. Our Lord's use of this proverb is positive, not negative. He said, "Do to men what you would like them to do to you." A very different thing from, "Don't do to other people what you don't want them to do to you." What would I like other people to do to me? Jesus says, "Well, don't wait; do it to them." I would like people to think of me as I really am before God. Well, think of them like that. I would really like people to give me credit for the generous motives I have. Well, give them credit for having them. I would really like that people should not pass harsh judgments on me, but that they should always understand that the one great motive of my life is to do them good. Well, have that attitude towards them. That is a maxim that Jesus wants us to have by us.

It is commonly used the other way, you find

it even in newspapers, "Don't do to others what you don't want them to do to you." But look at it the other way, "Do to other people as you wish them to do to you." If I have a feeling that I would like that person to pray for me; well, pray for that person. The measure of my growth in grace is my attitude towards others, and the Holy Ghost will kindle my imagination to picture many things I would like them to do to me; that is His way of telling you what to do to them. "Love your neighbor as yourself."

The devil comes as an angel of light and says, "You must not think about yourself." Well, if you don't, what can you make of that statement? The Holy Ghost will make you think about yourself. His only way of educating me when I am right with Him as to how to deal with other persons is making me picture what I would like those other persons to do to me, and then I go and do it to them. That is our Lord's measure for practical ethical conduct all through the Sermon on the Mount. No wonder men want to say His principles don't apply to this life, but to a future dispensation; but let us begin to work them out now.

(3) The Principal Meaning of Revelation. The principal meaning of revelation is that the

law of God may be incarnated in the believer— "Written epistles known and read of all men." This is the law that came through the prophets; for what purpose? That it might be manifested in your lives.

Jesus Christ came to make the great laws and principles of God incarnated in human life; not in good human life, but in bad human life. That is the miracle of Jesus Christ's grace, He did not put these things up as standards for us to come up to; He puts us in the place where He can remake us, and put the principles in us, and enable us to work them out by His guidance.

Study Number Six

MATTHEW SEVEN.

A. TWO GATES, TWO WAYS.
Matthew 7:13, 14.
1. "All Noble Things are Difficult."
2. "My Utmost for the Highest."
3. "A stoot heart tae a' stae brae."

B. TEST YOUR TEACHERS.
1. Possibility of Pretense.
Matthew 7: 15.
2. Place of Patience.
Matthew 7: 16.
3. Principle of Performance.
Matthew 7: 17, 18.
4. Power of Publicity.
Matthew 7: 19, 20.

C. APPEARANCE AND REALITY.
1. Recognize Men Without Labels.
Matthew 7: 21.
2. Remedy Mongers.
Matthew 7: 22.
3. Retributive Measures.
Matthew 7: 23.

D. THE TWO BUILDERS.
1. Spiritual Castles.
Matthew 7: 24.
2. Supreme Crisis.
Matthew 7: 25.
3. Suspicious Conditions.
Matthew 7: 26.
4. Supreme Catastrophe.
Matthew 7: 27.
5. Scriptural Concentration.

STUDY NUMBER SIX.

MATTHEW 7

The vital distinction between warning and threatening is just the difference between God and the devil. God never threatens, the devil never warns. Warning is a great, arresting statement of God's, inspired by His love and patience. The more you brood over that, the more you will find it throws a flood of light on the passages of the Old Testament in which God's warnings seem to be very strange, and of the New Testament where the statements of Jesus are so vivid, such as in Matthew 23.

Always remember that both the voice of God and of Jesus are divine voices, not human; there is no element of personal vindictiveness in them, no question of holding it, "If you don't do this, the consequences will fall on you." It is the great, patient love of God that puts the warnings, as much as to say, "Not this way." "The way of transgressors is hard," go behind that statement in your imagination, God is almost tender as He cannot make it easy; and God has made it difficult to go wrong, especially for His children.

A. TWO GATES, TWO WAYS. (Matt. 7:13, 14.)

Our Lord is using here an allegory that was perfectly familiar to all the people of His day, and He lifts it by His inspiration to embody His patient warning. Our Lord continually used proverbs and sayings that were familiar to His hearers, and put an altogether new meaning into them; and we now take three phrases that are quite familiar to us and which embody our Lord's thought.

(1) "All Noble Things are Difficult." Our Lord warns, in Matthew 7: 13, 14, that the devout life of a disciple is not a dream, but a decided discipline which calls for the use of all our powers. Note that no amount of determination can give me the new life of God, that is a gift; but the point of determination comes in letting that new life work itself out according to Christ's standard. We are always in danger of confounding what we can do and what we cannot do. At the beginning we try to save ourselves, we

try to sanctify ourselves, we try to give ourselves the Holy Spirit; all those things are utterly impossible. The only way we can get salvation, get sanctification, and get the Holy Spirit is by receiving them as gifts. The other snare is that we try to make out that God must make us "walk in the light." God does not, I must do the walking, He gives me the power to walk, but I must see that I use the power. So you find the confusion continually recurs, our trying to do what God alone can do, and then trying to make out that God will do what only we can do. Our Lord here in these warnings has indicated what we have to do, He has put the power and the life in us, He fills us with the Holy Spirit, now we have to work it out; that is, we have to realize that this noble life is gloriously difficult, not a difficulty that makes us faint and cave in, but a difficulty that rouses us up to overcome it.

(2) "My Utmost for the Highest." Our Lord emphasizes the need for us to keep our minds fixed on the straight way, *viz.*, as a disciple I will do my utmost as a proof that I appreciate God's utmost for me. How did Jesus live a holy life? He lived it by sacrificing Himself to His Father. How did He talk holy talking? By sacrificing His intellect to His Father. How did He work

holy working? By submitting His will to His Father. I have to use my utmost endeavors to do the same thing, and if I have the life of God I can do it. The motto over our side of the Gate of Life is, "All God's commands I can obey." Jesus, in John 14, puts that as the test of discipleship, "If you love me, you will keep my commandments," and you learn never to allow *I cannot* to creep in. "Oh, I am no saint, I cannot do this,"—those things must never come in, because if they do, we are a disgrace to Jesus Christ. "My utmost for the highest." Do I so appreciate the marvelous salvation of Jesus in saving and sanctifying me and filling me with the Holy Spirit that I do my utmost to be worthy of Him?

(3) "A stoot heart tae a' stae brae" (a strong heart to a difficult hill). In these verses our Lord warns us that the Christian life is a holy life, and that means we must not substitute the word *happy*. (Happiness we certainly will have, but it is a consequence of holiness.) Our Lord continually warns, without putting it in so many words, that we must never get off on the idea, which is exceedingly prevalent nowadays, of what we may safely call "the gospel of temperament," *viz.*, that we have to be happy and bright. All those are effects, they are not causes. Im-

mediately you make that the dominant characteristic of your life, "I am determined I will be happy and joyful," it will all go from you, because those things are not causes, they are not objects, they are consequences, things that follow without striving after them. Our Lord insists that we keep at one point, our eyes fixed on the one place, the strait gate and the narrow way, which means in my life, pure, holy living, and I will have happiness.

Note what our Lord says in the way of warning about worry in John 14; for instance, the words "Let not" are a command, and the words in practical Christianity mean "Worry is wicked." If you are going to keep this strong heart that God has given you to the difficult *braes* in life, you have continually to watch that one thing. You remember in the first parable our Lord gave, He said that "the cares of this life will choke my word in you," and you will find it is not the devil that first switches folks off Christ's way, it is the ordinary, steep difficulties of daily life; difficulties connected with money, with food, with clothing and situations. Remember Jesus Christ's warning that these things will choke all He puts in.

Look back on your own life, we have each had a place where the little worries have blotted God's face out, enfeebled our hearts and made us sorry and humiliated before Him, much more so than the times when we felt the temptation to sin. The temptation to sin finds something that makes us face it with vigor and earnestness, but the cares of this life, the *braes,* or difficulties, require the stout heart that God gives.

The whole summing up of this first great warning is twofold: it is easy to drift a little way, but it is easier to direct our steps in His way. Our Lord uses the illustration in Matthew 11, "Take my yoke upon you, and learn of me, for my yoke is easy and my burden is light." It seems amazingly difficult to put the yoke of Christ on, but immediately you do, it makes everything easy. It is much easier at the beginning apparently just simply to drift and say, "Oh, I can't"; but immediately you do, you find, blessed be the name of God, your heart and body and soul say, "I have the easiest way after all." Happiness and all these things attend, they are not my aim, my aim is the Lord Jesus Christ, and He has showered the *hundredfold* more on me all the way along.

B. TEST YOUR TEACHERS. (Matt. 7:15-20.)

Jesus warns His disciples to test preachers and teachers by their fruit. There are two ways of testing by fruit, one is by the fruit in the life of the preacher, and the other is by the fruit in the life of the doctrine. I may have a perfectly beautiful life in its fruits, but I may be teaching a doctrine which, if logically worked out, will produce the devil's fruit in other lives. Jesus says, "Test your teachers."

Without His warnings we are always captivated. It is the easiest thing in the world for us to be captivated by a beautiful life and say, "Now what that beautiful life teaches must be right." Jesus says, "Be careful, test your teacher by the fruit." The other side is just as true, that you may have teachers teaching beautiful truth whose doctrine in its fruit will be magnificent, but the fruit in their own lives is rotten. If we see a man with a beautiful life, we say his doctrine must be right, but not necessarily so; then we say because a man teaches the right thing, therefore his life is all right, not necessarily so. Test the doctrine by its fruit, and test the teacher by his fruit.

(1) Possibility of Pretence. (7:15.) Jesus would have us know that there are people who come clothed in the right doctrine, but inwardly their spirit is the spirit of Satan. The very allowing of my mind to think that it is possible to

pretend is quite sufficient warning. Jesus says, "Beware of the possibility of pretence." Immediately the disciples' eyes are off Jesus, pious pretending follows instantly. 1 John 1:7 is the essential condition for all saints. You find, as you study the Sermon on the Mount, that you are *badgered* by the Spirit of God from every standpoint but one, and it is the standard of a child depending on God. Immediately we depend on anything else, there comes in this possibility of pretence, pious pretence, not hypocritical; we are dealing with pretence, the desperately sincere effort to be right when we know we are not. A hypocrite is something infinitely more than that, a hypocrite is one who tries and succeeds in living a twofold life for his own ends. Our Lord is describing dangerous teachers here.

(2) Place of Patience. (7:16.) Our Lord in some cases would have us *bide our time.* This warning is against over-zealousness on the part of heresy-hunters. An incident in the life of our Lord points out what I mean. John and another disciple came to Jesus and said: "We saw a man casting out devils, and as he did not come with us we forbade him." Jesus said, "Don't, no man can do these things and speak lightly of me." Take heed that we do not make

carnal suspicion take the place of the discernment of the Spirit. Fruit, and fruit alone, is the test, not the disciples' fancy. If I see distinctly in a minister or a Sunday-school teacher or a fellow-Christian the fruit in the life showing itself like thistles, then Jesus said, "Now you know perfectly well there is the wrong root there, you do not gather a thistle off any other root than a thistle-root"; but it is quite possible to mistake in the winter time a rose tree for a weed, unless you are thoroughly expert in judging, so there is a place for patience, and the Lord would have us heed it.

Wait for the fruit to manifest itself and don't be guided by fancy. It is an easy business to get alarmed and to persuade myself that my conviction is the standard of Christ. Immediately I do, I condemn everyone to perdition who does not agree with me, I am obliged to, because my conviction has taken in me the place of Jesus Christ. God's Book never says, "Walk in the light of my conviction," but "Walk in the light of the Lord." You have to make a vital distinction between the people who object to my way of presenting God's Gospel and the people who object to God's Gospel. There are ever so many people who object to my way of presenting the truth, but they certainly do not object to God making them holy, and I have to make the distinction clear, I have to remember that the difficulty in presenting the truth has been with me, not with God.

(3) Principle of Performance. (7: 17, 18.) If I wish the performances of my life to be steadily holy, I must be holy in the principle of my life. If I am to bring forth good fruit, I must have a good root. Just as it is possible for a man in a flying-machine to imitate a bird, so it is possible to imitate the fruit of the Spirit. The vital difference is the same in both, the aeroplane cannot persist, it can only fly spasmodically, there is no principle of life behind; and my imitation of the Spirit requires certain things that keep me from the public gaze and then I can imitate fairly well; but if I am going to bring forth the performance and fruit that is right, I must have the principle inside right. I must know what it is to be born again of the Holy Ghost, and sanctified, and filled with the Holy Spirit, then my performance will bring the fruit. Fruit is clearly expounded in the Epistles and is quite distinct from gifts or from the manifest seal of God on His own Word.

(4) Power of Publicity. (7: 19, 20.) Our Lord in His own life lived most publicly. When standing before Caiaphas He said, "I spake nothing in private" (John 18:20), and our Lord here

applies the same test of publicity to His disciples. All through the life of our Lord the one thing that made His enemies *mad* was the manner in which He did things, they were annoyed at His miracles because they manifested His public power. People are annoyed at the same things to-day, they are annoyed at public testimony. Jesus makes publicity the test, that is, there is no use saying, "Oh, yes, I live a holy life, but I don't say anything about it"; then you certainly don't, for the two go together. Our Lord warns that the men who won't be conspicuous as His disciples will be made to be conspicuous as His enemies.

Whenever a thing has its root in the heart of God, it wants to be public, it wants to get out, it must do things in the external and the open, and Jesus Christ not only encouraged it, but He insisted on it, both for bad and for good. Things must be dragged out, it is God's law, men cannot hide what they really are, and if they are His disciples, it will be publicly portrayed.

Our Lord said, in Matthew 10, that men like wolves will want to devour you if you publicly perform or testify, but do not hide your light under a bushel for fear of wolfish men who can only destroy your body, but be careful that you do not go contrary to your duty and have your soul destroyed; be as "wise as serpents and harmless as doves." That warning of the Lord needs to come back here, that we have simply to wait in patience; if there are certain men and women who are not living in the public, conspicuous lives as the saints of God, as sure as God is on His throne, the inevitable principle must work, the public exposure of them. If we are not publicly conspicuous in the good, we will be publicly conspicuous in the bad.

C. APPEARANCE AND REALITY. (Matt. 7: 21-23.)

Our Lord here makes the test of goodness not only good intention but carrying out God's will.

(1) Recognize Men Without Labels. (7:21.) Human nature is very fond of labels, that means the counterfeit of confession. It is so easy to be branded with labels, so easy in a certain stage to wear a *bonnet* or a *ribbon*, it is much easier to do that than to confess. Our Lord Jesus never used the word *testimony*, He used a much more testing word, He used the word *confess*. Our Lord said that the test of goodness was confession by doing the will of God. Therefore if the disciple is to discern between the man with the

label and the man with the *goods*, he must have the spirit of discernment, *viz.*, the Holy Spirit. The label and the goods ought to go together, but our Lord is warning His disciples that there are times when they do not. A good many of us before we get right with God like to say, "Oh, yes, I quite agree with that, I don't think anyone ought to wear a badge." Jesus says, "If you don't confess me before men, I will not confess you before my father," and immediately you confess you must have a badge, and if you don't put one on yourself, they will put one on you. Watch what Jesus says about discipleship, you must be conspicuous, and the old cunning, carnal mind comes in and says we must live the holy life and say nothing about it. That is absolutely contrary to the spirit of the New Testament. Our Lord here is warning that it is possible for a man to carry the "label" without the goods, that is, it is possible for men to wear the badge of being "my disciple" while they are not.

(2) Remedy Mongers. (7:22.) Our Lord here warns against those who utilize His words and His ways to remedy the evils of men while they are disloyal to Jesus. "Many will say to me in that day, Lord, Lord, have we not prophesied in Thy name? and in Thy name have cast out de-

vils? and in Thy name have done many wonderful works?" Not one word of confession of Jesus, one thing only, and that is, we have preached Him as a remedy, like quack preachers. The test of discipleship, as Jesus is dealing with it in this chapter, is fruit in goodly character, and the disciple is warned not to be blinded by the fact that God honors His Word even when it is preached from contention and the wrong motive. (See Phil. 1: 15.) We have all had puzzles with the thing that is indicated in this statement of Jesus, we start out with the honest, plain, simple truth that the labels and the goods must go together, they ought to go together, but Jesus is warning here that sometimes they get severed, and you sometimes find cases in which God honors His Word and the people who preach it are not living a right life. Now He says if you are going to judge the preachers, judge them by their fruit. He gave the same warning in Luke 10 to His own disciples. They were delighted because the very devils were subject to them, and Jesus said, "Don't rejoice in that I gave you power, but rejoice that your names are written in the Book of Life." We are back to the one point—right relationship to Jesus Christ, unsullied in every way, in every detail, private and public.

(3) Retributive Measures. (7: 23.) In these solemn words Jesus states that He has to confess to some Bible expositors, some prophetic students, some workers of miracles, that they must depart from Him for they have twisted the ways of God and made them unequal, that is the meaning of the word "iniquity" (twisted out of the straight). We are continually perplexed by people who are preaching the right thing and who are proving that God is blessing the preaching, and yet all the time the Spirit of God is warning, "No! No!! No!!!" Only as we rely on and recognize the Spirit of God do we discern how Jesus Christ's warnings work. Never trust the best man or woman you ever met, trust only the Lord Jesus Christ. That holds good all the way along, "Lean not to your own understanding, put not your trust in princes, put not your trust in anyone." Have you ever noticed that every (not some) character in God's Book, when that character is taken as a guide, leads away from God? We are never told to follow in all the footsteps of the saints, we are only told to follow in the footsteps of the saints in so far as they have obeyed God. "Keep right with me, keep in the light," says Jesus, and you have fellowship with one another, that is with everyone

else in the light. All our panics, moral, intellectual and spiritual, come just on that point, whenever we take our eyes off Jesus Christ, we get startled. "There is another one gone down, I did think he would stand right." "Look at Me," says Jesus.

D. THE TWO BUILDERS. (Matt. 7: 24-29.)

The emphasis of our Lord is laid here on hearing and doing these sayings of mine. It would be a profitable study if we would hunt up what Jesus has to say about hearing. "He that hath ears to hear"—it would throw an amount of light on how I have heard what He said.

(1) Spiritual Castles. (7: 24.) Our buildings must be conspicuous, and the test of the spiritual building is not its fair beauty but its foundation and bulwarks. Look at the most beautiful spiritual fabrics which are raised in the shape of books and lives, beautiful and full of the finest diction and statements spiritual and good; but when the test comes, down they go. What is the test? They have not been built on "these sayings of mine," that is, they are built altogether in the air, with no foundation.

(2) Supreme Crisis. (7: 25.) Every spiritual castle will be tested by a threefold storm: rain, flood and wind—the world, the flesh, and

the devil, and it will only stand if it is founded on these sayings of mine.

(3) Suspicious Conditions. (7: 26.) Every spiritual fabric that is built with the sayings of Jesus instead of being founded on them, Jesus calls a building by foolish men. "He that heareth these sayings of mine and doeth them." There is a tendency in everyone of us to appreciate with our intellects and even with our spirits and hearts the teachings of Jesus, but if we refuse to do them, everything we build will go by the foundation when the test comes. Paul applies this when he says, "If I build hay, wood or stubble, gold or silver, it has all to be tested by the supreme test."

(4) Supreme Catastrophe. (7: 27.) All that I build will be tested supremely and it will tumble in a fearful disaster unless it is built on the sayings of Jesus. It is an easy business to build with the sayings of Jesus, to sling texts of Scripture together and build them into any kind of fabric you like. Jesus did not say he that builds with my statements, but he that builds on them the character of home life, of business life. Did you ever notice the repulsion that the healthy saint and the healthy worldling have against any man or woman who tries to build with the state-

ments of Jesus? You will find that God brings the pagan and the saint before this tremendous standard, "What about your actions?" These things are quoted in your office, in your homes, but how do you work them out? That is what Jesus is saying, it is only when it is built on my statements, that is, our Lord makes no allowance for having some compartments holy and other compartments not, the whole thing must be radically built on the foundation.

(5) Scriptural Concentration. (7:28, 29.) The summing up is a descriptive note inspired by the Spirit of God on the way in which people who heard Jesus had forgotten everything else but His doctrine. Its application for us is not what would Jesus do, but what did Jesus say. As I concentrate on what He said, so I can stake my immortal soul on those statements.

THE END.